Unexpected Assassins

Accidental Mobster
Book 4

Daisy Emory

This book is to all of my fans who have supported me over the years. THANK YOU for giving this unknown author a chance and reading this series.

Chapter 1

Erina

"If you try to stop me, I'm going to castrate each and every one of you. I am going to leave for my girls' weekend," I reminded my husbands. "So, you better keep your men in line. I don't have time for any shenanigans." None outside of what me and my best friends would get up to anyway.

My three husbands, seated at the conference table looking over plans for some new operation, finally looked up at me.

"What? What do you mean you're leaving?" Connor, the boss of the Gregori Mafia, my first husband, and a complete hot head, asked. His green eyes narrowed and his red hair seemed to wave in the breeze from the air conditioner. He was on the shorter side, but muscular, and trained in mixed martial arts to ensure he could hold his own against professional fighters and assassins. The smug pain in my butt had even entered a few MMA tournaments just to test his abilities... and won.

"That starts today?" Alexi, the best assassin in our mafia and one of the best kissers on the planet, asked with a scowl. He was the shortest and thinnest of my three husbands, which made him perfect for fitting into small places to pull off incredible assassinations.

"Yes. I've reminded you boys a dozen times and put it on all of your calendars," I huffed. I pointed to the wall where our monthly calendar hung. "It's right there."

Alexi and Connor turned to look at the calendar.

Blain kept his eyes on me and smirked. His rugged face was covered in dark stubble about as long as his shaved head. His jaw was just overdue for a shave, while he kept his head shaved so no one could grab his hair during a fight. He was the muscle of the three, tall, buff, and a great fighter. Getting thrown around by him was one of my favorite activities.

Blain was the only one who had remembered, which was typical. Despite Connor being the brains, Blain was the one who had an amazing memory.

"I can't believe you're still going," Connor muttered as he turned back around.

"They are my best friends and we, *I*, need a break. It's been non-stop mafia business for months. If I don't get out of this house and laugh with my friends, I'm going to start murdering people."

"I don't like you going without one of us," Alexi said as he turned back to face me.

I sat on the edge of the table and smiled. These three were over protective alphas to a T. They usually kept me locked in this mansion and didn't even like other men looking at me.

It had taken months for them to agree to let one of my best friends, Amelia, come and spend the night at our place. And they'd only agreed to it as long as none of Amelia's men came. Though, I did understand that a bit since she was part of a different mafia.

Letting me leave for a night was one of their biggest fears and had been only possible with me agreeing to stay at one of our co-owned casinos.

"Letting me leave is always hard on you guys, but I always come back fine. Besides, I'll be surrounded by our security, and I know you hot jerks are going to be checking the video feeds to keep an eye on me," I said in a playful tone. After dating these men for two years and marrying them three years ago, I was well aware of what I'd signed up for and how they were. They weren't watching me because they worried I would do something they didn't like. They were watching me to see if they needed to come and rescue me.

To be fair to them, I had needed rescuing a time or two when rival mafias were trying to start shit.

Thankfully, that didn't happen often and nothing awful had happened. Well, to me. Those other mafias had been obliterated.

"I still don't like it," Connor grumbled.

"I know, baby," I replied with a smile.

They knew there was no talking me out of it. They could grumble and whine, but at the end of the day, I was going.

"I'm surprised Brian is letting his wife go," Connor said, shaking his head, "with what he's got going on in his territory."

"It's because of what's going on that he's letting her go," I explained. "Their battles and security breaches are making him more and more nervous about her safety, so letting her come into our joint territory is one of the safest places for her."

"Did Stephan ever get back to us?" Alexi asked. "I know they were having some issues, too."

"They're doing a lot better than Brian," I answered.

Connor sighed. "Fine. Fine. We'll behave, so you don't have to cut your time short. Will you wear the necklace?"

The necklace he was talking about had a tracking chip in it. It looked pretty and normal, so most wouldn't think to remove it if they kidnapped me.

I walked over and kissed his cheek. "Yes. Amelia will be wearing her tracking ring, too."

Amelia's husbands were just as overprotective as mine, possibly more so.

"You send us an emergency text the minute anything goes wrong, you understand?"

I saluted him. "Yes, boss!"

Connor's jaw clenched. He *hated* when I called him boss.

Chuckling, I kissed him again. "I promise." My smile dropped and I said, "I need a distraction while you are all at the Mafia Weekend." Mafia Weekend was when all of the mafia bosses in the country gathered to discuss agreements and issues as well as any federal investigations the others should be aware of.

"I'll come with you and help you finish packing," Blain said, standing from his chair.

Connor waved his hand, dismissing him.

We walked out of the meeting room, exiting through a secret wall that only we knew about, and entered Connor's second office. We walked out and continued down the hallway, side by side, until we reached my bedroom.

"You sure you can't postpone?" Blain asked softly and shut the door behind him.

"There will always be mafia trouble. I *need* this vacation, Blain. I'm going stir crazy."

He hugged me and kissed me lightly on the lips. "I could think of a few things to help ease your stir craziness."

I snickered. "I bet you could, but that's only a temporary fix."

He arched a brow. "Are you challenging me?"

Pushing against his chest, I put distance between us. "I'm going and that's that."

He raised his hands up in defeat. "Fine. Fine. I will drop the topic."

"Yes, let's switch the topic to a more important one. Are you sure that everything is baby proofed at my parents' and she won't hit her head on anything? Did you make sure to have the drawer locks installed and the front door lock moved to the top and—"

Before I could finish my questions, Blain wrapped his arms around me and kissed my forehead. "Darling, I have followed every single one of your directions down to the letter. If you're so worried about Melina, maybe you should stay home?"

I pushed back from him immediately, a scowl scrunching my forehead. "I am *not* staying home. I have earned this vacation. It's only one night and you'll be nearby the casino anyways." As much as I worried about Melina, my six-month-old baby girl, I needed a break. It sounded awful to say out loud, to voice that I needed time away from her, but I'd been cooped up in the mansion since I was five months pregnant. I'd barely gotten Connor to agree to let Marlee and Amelia visit me to meet Melina a month after her birth. So, even if it made me feel like a bad mother, I was going to take the night away and enjoy myself.

My parents were going to watch her for the weekend and they were extremely devoted grandparents. Dad had a dozen guards and three of his most trusted would be with Melina and them at all times. Dad was also one of the best marksmen I'd ever met. He had been trained by the military and continued to hone his skills to this day; he even had a shooting range on his property.

I was so excited to finally pack my suitcase for the trip. I carefully laid out my clothes on my bed, making sure to choose outfits that were both cute and comfortable, and made sure I grabbed the dress that I'd purchased specifically for tonight. Amelia and Marlee would have the dresses I'd picked out for them as well. I decided to bring a pair of jeans and a sweater for the return day. I also packed a flowy sundress for the next afternoon, along with a pair of sandals and some jewelry to dress it up. As backups, I packed a pair of shorts and a t-shirt. Remembering we had the spa, I also added my swimsuit and a beach cover-up. In addition to my clothes, I packed a few essential toiletries, including my toothbrush, toothpaste, and hairbrush. I also brought a small makeup bag with some basic cosmetics, like mascara and lip balm. Finally, I zipped up my suitcase and hoisted it off the bed, feeling a sense of anticipation and excitement for the weekend ahead. I couldn't wait to spend some quality time with my girlfriends and make some fun memories together.

Chapter 2

Marlee

"Are you certain you still want me to go?" I asked Brian, my husband and Boss of the Toretto Mafia.

We stood in his office, looking over some plans for the new hotel we wanted to build in the outskirts of a prosperous part of the city. Luckily, despite all the craziness elsewhere in our lives, the hotel development was going smoothly and contractors were signed on, and at decent prices.

There had been a few tiny hiccups, but nothing that we hadn't been able to squash and make disappear relatively quickly. Well before the media got wind about it.

He smiled and gently gripped my upper arms, turning me away from the documents. His eyes were full of love as he looked at me, something that had taken me about a decade to truly accept, and now it was what kept me steady. No matter what life threw at us, we were partners, equals, best friends, and would survive together. "You can't come with me, and you and I both know you'll be safer with Amelia and Erina in that casino than even here in our mansion."

The casino had guards paid by the mafia, so it was definitely the safest place. Plus, I didn't want to stay cooped up in this house when my two besties would be drinking and enjoying time together.

"Since when did you become the pragmatic one?" I teased and rubbed the tip of my nose against his.

He kissed my lips lightly and exhaled. "You know I'll be worried the whole time, but I have learned to relax quite a bit in the past two years."

What he hadn't added was that it was thanks to Amelia and the Moriarty Mafia. That woman had done a lot for us, and I was proud to call her one of my best friends.

"Well, I suppose I better finish packing then," I said, kissed his cheek, and went to my room.

As I walked into my bedroom, my eyes were drawn to the queen-sized, four poster bed with burgundy silk sheets, more pillows than anyone needed, and a pink and sparkly princess canopy over the top. I'd joked about always wanting one as a child, so when we'd designed the room, Brian had gotten it for me. To the right of the bed, a large floor-to-ceiling window looked out onto my sprawling estate, which was bathed in the warm glow of the afternoon sun. A set of heavy velvet curtains were drawn to the side, allowing the light to flood in and fill the room with a sunlight. On the opposite side of the room, a sleek and polished mahogany dresser stood tall. Its smooth surface was adorned with an array of elegant crystal perfume bottles, gleaming silver brushes, and other beauty essentials, most gifts from Brian and my family.

Above the dresser hung an ornate gilt-framed mirror, reflecting the opulence of the room back at me. As a child, this is exactly how I'd pictured my dream room, and it was finally reality. In one corner, a sumptuous armchair and ottoman were arranged around a small table with a few books I'd recently been reading. That was my favorite spot to curl up with a book and a cup of tea, enjoying the peace and quiet of my private sanctuary. As I made my way around the room, I couldn't help but feel a sense of satisfaction and contentment. This was my own personal oasis, a haven of comfort and luxury that Brian and I had created together.

Unlike most couples, we had separate bedrooms. Some thought it was a sign that we'd had a falling out or that we didn't actually like each other, but that was the furthest thing from the truth. The issue was that I snored, a lot, and it kept Brian awake at night because he was a light sleeper. So, on nights where I knew for sure I'd be snoring or when he had a big meeting or event the following day, we slept in separate beds. It was also nice to have an area to decompress from time to time when we did have a fight. Thankfully, that wasn't often.

My phone chimed with Erina's personalized ringtone. I answered the video call and set the phone in the phone stand on my dresser to continue packing. "Hello, beautiful momma."

"The eagle has left the roost!" she shouted and fist pumped the air a few times.

"We can still turn this car around," Alexi threatened from the background of her call.

"Not if you value your dangling bits remaining dangling," she grumbled.

Oh, yeah. She definitely needed a vacation. After having

the baby, it had been nearly impossible to visit her. In fact, we'd only been able to visit her in person once. I was fairly certain the only reason that had happened was because Amelia kept threatening to break in if she wasn't let in.

We had both witnessed Erina's declining mental state via our video calls, and although one in person visit didn't cure her, it did help. Even Connor couldn't argue that. He just didn't want to admit that Erina needed more than her husbands in her life now. He didn't want to admit that there might be something he couldn't do for his wife.

"Why haven't you left yet?" Erina asked as she brought the phone closer to her face, so she could see what I was doing. "Please tell me you aren't backing out."

"Don't worry, you don't get to party without me. I'm just finishing packing right now."

"Are things that bad?" she asked softly.

There was a new gang that moved into our territory and try as we might, we couldn't eradicate them. They messed with our supply chains, killed our people, convinced some of our people to defect to their side, and were a huge issue. It didn't make sense for a new gang to have so much strength, and we were pretty sure they were funded by a separate rival mafia, but hadn't been able to find the proof yet. I thought Angel Eyes might be involved, since he had been over on this side of the country recently, but no one had seen him and we couldn't find any sign of him. The worst part about the new group was that they had started to attack us at the mansion. Our safe haven was under assault, and I was constantly on edge.

That was why Brian wanted me to leave. He wanted me someplace safer while he was gone as well.

Being in the same city would make us both feel better.

I finished folding the dress in my hands and smiled at her. "We'll get by," I said in as chipper a tone as I could. "Have you talked to Amelia yet?"

She sighed. "She didn't answer."

"Don't worry, you know she will come, even if she has to fight her own husbands to get to us."

Amelia was a whirlwind of smiles, joy, and pandemonium. Her charm and chaos were somehow endearing and frightful all at the same time, which was what made people love her.

Never in my life had I expected to not only join hands with the Moriarty Mafia, but the Gregori Mafia, too. Most surprising of all, I had never expected to become friends with another mafia wife.

Normally, a mafia wife's life was solitary, aside from the mafia family. Even those like Amelia and Erina who had multiple spouses rarely had friends outside of their mafia. It was a closed circle, one that didn't allow for outsiders who could possibly break their trust and hurt them.

Amelia shattered all of that and made our lives better... *so* much better. She showed us a life that I had only ever dreamed of.

One where I was going on a weekend getaway to a casino for food, drinks, and fun with my two best friends.

Chapter 3

Amelia

"I will stab you right in the balls if you don't stop rushing!" I shouted into my headset.

Dane choked on his beer and Forrest patted his back roughly to help dislodge the misplaced alcohol.

"Don't get that on my carpet," I ordered him before focusing back on the videogame I was currently playing.

Arcadio had introduced me to a new videogame that had an adorable woman in a mech that could send the mech to explode when she got enough kills. I'd become obsessed with the game and spent quite a few hours playing, grinding my way to the top of the ranks, and collecting every skin, aka outfit, for the character I could.

Dane and Forrest had come into my room to watch me play games and be near me. It'd become a ritual for us at least once every other week. The two friends sat on my bed, beers in hand, and whispered to each other so as not to distract me.

Poor Stephan had been slammed with issues from our mafia side of the business, having to send Shea and Arcadio out to deal with issues that needed a... rougher hand. So, he was rarely able to come in and experience my videogame shenanigans and rants.

"Regroup," Hunter, my bodyguard and a former MMA fighter, ordered the team in his headset with a stern voice.

Since I'd been spending most of my time on the game, and he'd been bored just standing guard, Stephan had ordered a gaming laptop for him to play with me, too.

It was honestly one of the best ideas Stephan had had.

Expectedly, he'd chosen a brawler type character.

"Oh, sure they listen to you," I said, and begrudgingly joined him as the team grouped up with him.

Five minutes later, more frustrated than I'd been in days, I put my headset down and blew out a breath.

"You got endorsements," Forrest said, trying to make me feel better.

I scoffed. "Of course I did. I actually played the game properly." I wasn't great at the game by any means, but I did my job as the tank and tried to keep others alive, and take the brunt of the damage.

"You were supposed to leave... five minutes ago," Dane advised me with a smirk after looking up from his phone.

My mouth dropped and I smacked his arm. "You should have warned me!" Rushing around, I hurried to finish packing. Picking up my phone, I shrieked at the missed calls on my phone from Erina and Marlee. "Shit. Shit. Shit."

"You could just stay home," Forrest offered, sliding his hands around my hips to my stomach.

I smacked his hand. "Bad husband! We've been planning this for a year. I am not staying home. Besides, you all are going to Mafia Weekend. I'll just be stewing in worry all alone."

"Not all alone," Hunter grumbled.

"Shadows are supposed to be silent," I said, though we both knew I didn't mean it. Hunter had quickly become a very close friend, almost sibling, and we spent more time than was even necessary together, much to my husbands' chagrin.

He mimicked me silently as he stood and stretched.

Dane asked, "Do you have your—"

I interrupted him, knowing what he was about to ask. "Yes, I have my tracker on, and I won't take it off. Not even when swimming or showering. Promise."

"And you're going to be extra careful, right?" Forrest asked.

"Hunter is going to be with me, remember?" That had taken some negotiating with my besties' husbands, since we were going to their hotel and they weren't sending personal guards with them.

"He's already gotten the nagging lecture," Hunter said.

Forrest and Dane narrowed their eyes.

"I mean... the *instructions* from your adoring and not at all overbearing husbands," Hunter amended with a smile.

"You've spent too much time with Amelia," Forrest said and shook his head with a chuckle.

"What's that supposed to mean?" I demanded, hands on hips, and suitcase forgotten.

"It means, lovely wife, that you are a unique and boisterous personality," Stephan said. Stephan Moriarty, billionaire, voted sexiest man alive four years in a row, and in an insane twist to my life, one of my husbands. I was one of the luckiest people in the universe. He leaned his shoulder against the doorframe and smiled, his eyes crinkling slightly at the sides as he looked at me with a warmth that made my heart soar.

"Did Mom show up yet?" I asked.

My mother and her boyfriends were going to watch the children while we were all gone for the weekend. She had been away for over six months, so she was very excited to see her grandchildren again.

"She's almost here," Stephan answered. "She said to make sure you were gone before she got here, so you wouldn't try to distract her with instructions on keeping them alive, since she clearly had kept you alive, or wanting attention as her daughter, since she now has grandbabies that are the most important people in her life and you should accept that you have now taken a backseat."

My mother was a smart ass, and I was unsurprised to hear she had said something like that. I also knew she had said it lovingly and it was part of how our relationship worked. We teased each other and said things that others would think cruel, but it was really lighthearted banter. When called upon, she would come help me immediately and I knew she loved me just as much as I loved her.

"I'm almost done packing. I just need to find my bikini," I said, spinning away from all the men staring at me, and hurried to my walk-in closet to try to find where I had thrown it the last time I had washed it.

Having a maid would have simplified our lives, but I actually liked doing the laundry, and the guys used it as bonding time with me. They took turns helping put the clothes away, chatting about random things while we folded socks and sorted the piles. Sometimes we got into playful fights throwing the clean clothes at each other or snapping butts with the tips of the towels we were folding, which added to our bonding experience.

We were weird billionaires, that was for sure.

Stephan stepped around me, bent, opened the second drawer of the third shelf, and held up my bikini top. As soon as I took it from his hand, he spun around to the other side of the closet, opened the top, middle drawer, and pulled out my bikini bottoms.

My mouth dropped. "Did you separate them on purpose so I couldn't find them?"

He arched a brow and looked down at me. "You think I would do something so petty?"

He definitely wouldn't do something petty, but I didn't have another explanation at the moment.

"Well, how do you explain this?" I asked.

He set his hand on my cheek and smiled. "You, Darling. I watched you put them away, each item on a different day in the different drawers, and knew I needed to keep the memory at the forefront of my mind because you would forget where you put them."

I returned his smile and hugged him. "I could kiss you right now!"

Stephan's biggest secret from the world was that he was asexual. He wasn't aromantic, thankfully, and though we held hands, cuddled, and on occasion kissed, I still liked to ensure I respected his boundaries.

He bent down and kissed me lightly on the lips. "I'll accept your reward."

"Your phone is ringing again," Dane called.

I yelped, spun away from Stephan, and raced out to answer. "I'm coming! I'm coming!" I shouted as I hit accept.

"Ew, TMI," Erina said.

I snorted. "Like I'd answer the phone, even for you, if I were having sex."

"Please don't," she said with a chuckle, and I heard one of her husbands laugh in the background.

"I'm leaving in five minutes," I promised.

"Give my niece and nephew a hug from me before you leave," she ordered.

I saluted her with the hand holding my bikini, even though she couldn't see me, earning smirks and my husbands shaking their heads at me. "Yes, ma'am."

"Hurry up!" she ordered and hung up.

I tossed my bikini into the bag and zipped it closed. Immediately, I realized I hadn't packed my toiletries bag. "Toothbrush!" I yelled, and hurried to my bathroom to grab the bag from under the sink which held a toothbrush, travel toothpaste, deodorant, lotion, and pain medicine in case I got cramps.

Forrest unzipped my bag, rifled through it, and said, "Hairbrush, too."

I spun, one foot in the air, back into the bathroom to grab my hairbrush.

"She needs pajama pants," Forrest told Dane.

Dane walked to my dresser and pulled out two pairs of

my fleece pajama pants as I tossed my toiletries and hairbrush into the bag.

"Shoes!" I yelped and turned to go to my closet, but Stephan was already behind me, a pair of sexy high heels and a pair of flip flops in his hand.

"You'll probably want this, too," Forrest said and carried out the dress Erina had ordered for me to wear to dinner.

"Oh!" I gasped. "Erina would have been so mad if I'd left that behind."

Normally, I wasn't quite so scatterbrained, but with my increased responsibilities on the mafia side and requests for upgraded models of the mirror I'd created for our business side, I was constantly busy. So busy that I rarely took lunch breaks, choosing to eat during meetings, or while in brainstorming sessions with my teams.

"That's why you have us," Dane said, and hugged me from behind. "To keep you from forgetting important things that would upset your friends."

"I hope that's not the only reason I have you," I replied in a teasing tone.

He spun me around and kissed me deeply. "Definitely not the only reason."

I rested my head on his chest and looked over at Stephan and Forrest. "Promise me that you'll be extra careful this weekend, too? I know you're all supposed to be on neutral terms during Mafia Weekend, but it still worries me."

We had an alliance with the Torreto Mafia and the Gregori Mafia, but others weren't fond of us.

Plus, all the trouble we'd caused in Scotland, and with

what Angel Eyes had caused here, I couldn't stop the wriggling vine of worry in the back of my mind.

"We will be extra careful," Forrest promised and pulled me away from Dane to hug me.

"When do you guys leave?" I asked from within Forrest's muscular and warm arms.

"After your mother gets here," Stephan answered. "Now, go say goodbye to Shea and Arcadio before you leave."

"Babies first!" I said, and rushed off to the living room, where I knew Arcadio was playing with Callen and Paige.

We'd had to increase our baby proofing on the rooms that the kids were allowed in because they were walking and trying to climb on everything. I stepped over the baby gate and picked up Callen, who was the closest, giving him a tight hug. His hair was still short and fine, and it tickled my nose as I squeezed him.

"Mamama," he mumbled, and patted me with one hand.

"Momma is going to miss you," I said, kissed the top of his head, and set him down.

Paige opened and closed her hands at me from where she sat on the floor, wanting to get picked up, too. I obliged, picking her up and hugging and kissing her also.

They were growing up so fast, and I desperately wished for more time with them. Thankfully, since their daycare was at our office, I was able to go down and visit during breaks or on lunches sometimes. It still wasn't enough.

"We need a family vacation," I told Paige, who patted my upper chest while babbling baby nonsense.

"I agree," Arcadio said as he stood. His wavy black hair was pulled back into a ponytail and I enjoyed being able to see his handsome face fully. He stalked towards me, lithe and graceful from all his years as an assassin.

Slowly, I set Paige on the floor with her brother, stepping around her to reach Arcadio. "Do I get a kiss before I leave?" I set my hands on his chest, leaned into him a bit, and fluttered my eyelashes.

He leaned down, brushed his warm lips against mine, and started to straighten.

I threw my arms around his neck, forcing him back down, and claimed his mouth with mine. His tongue slid across mine, tasting of cinnamon, his favorite gum flavor.

His hands slid around my waist, pulling me against his firm, muscular body, and I moaned softly.

"Get a room," my mother ordered from right behind me.

I yelped and leapt away from Arcadio, falling onto the couch behind me.

Mom smirked, proud of herself for sneaking up on us. "Hello, Daughter."

"Mom," I huffed, smoothing my clothes as I stood. "You're rude."

Arcadio hugged Mom and then shooed me. "Get out of here or I'll keep you."

"Love you," I called over my shoulder as I ran out of the room. "Take care of my babies!"

"Will do," Mom called back, already holding both Paige and Callen in her arms, making noises and funny faces at them so that they would laugh.

I turned the corner of the hallway and ran into a large wall of warm flesh and muscle.

"Just who I was looking for!" I said and wrapped my arms around him without looking up.

Shea hugged me back, his arms engulfing me. "Are you sure you want to go?"

"Yes," I replied immediately.

He picked me up, large hands wrapping almost all the way around my waist, forcing me to wrap my legs around him. He dropped his hands to my butt, holding me up easily.

The new position brought us eye to eye, allowing me to kiss him and then rub my face against his like a cat. "Keep Stephan and the others safe, okay?" I whispered. "I've got a bad feeling about Mafia Weekend."

"You focus on keeping yourself safe," he ordered me.

I nodded and laid my cheek against his shoulder. "I'll be careful."

"And you'll wear your tracker?" he asked as he walked me towards the garage.

"Every second," I promised, leaned up, and gave him a scout's salute.

He didn't smile like I thought he would, just nodded once.

Shea, aka The Ox, was stoic a lot in public, but normally at home he was soft and kind. He must have been incredibly stressed.

I hugged him tightly. "I love you, Oxie Loxie."

"I love you, too. More than you'll ever know."

Finally at the door, he set me down and I grabbed my luggage, which sat beside Hunter's. Hunter stood there, looking bored.

"Ready?" Hunter asked, and took the two bags outside without a word.

My hand hung in the air, having previously been holding the bag.

Shea hugged me, pulling me out of my shock. "Have a fun time."

I hugged him back. "Keep everyone safe."

"Always," he said, kissing the top of my head.

I sauntered out of the door and climbed into the driver's seat of my car. "You're grumpy today."

Hunter ignored me, buckling his seatbelt and unlocking his cell phone to play one of his various games.

"Alright, time to go! I'm already late and will get nagged at for sure." I'd just supplicate her with booze, and she'd forgive me.

Chapter 4

Amelia

The hotel was busy, as usual, but none of that mattered since I was a VIP. The valet took my car key and Hunter carried our bags inside.

As I walked through the grand entrance of the casino hotel, I was immediately struck by the glittering lights and the lively sounds of slot machines ringing in the background. The lobby was bustling with people, and the energy was palpable.

The high ceilings and elegant chandeliers gave the room an air of sophistication and luxury. To my left, I could see a large seating area where people were relaxing and socializing. Plush sofas and armchairs were arranged around low tables, creating an inviting space to sit and unwind. To my right was a bar, where a bartender was expertly crafting cocktails for a group of patrons. The bar was made of sleek black marble and was adorned with rows of liquor bottles, making it a visually striking focal point in the lobby. As I looked around the lobby, I noticed several shops and restaurants lining the perimeter of the space. The scent of freshly baked pastries wafted from a nearby bakery, and I could hear the sounds of laughter and conversation emanating from a nearby restaurant. Overall, the lobby of the casino hotel was a bustling and vibrant space, filled with excitement and energy. The darkened entrance doors made it impossible to tell what time of day it was outside, which was exactly what the casino wanted. It helped trick people into thinking they hadn't spent much time at all there, giving away their money to the slots and tables.

We didn't need to check in, since Erina was already here, so we walked straight towards the elevators, bypassing the giant black, polished wood check-in counter staffed by gorgeous women with warm, inviting smiles.

A large man in a suit with a neck full of tattoos, and dark black glasses got into the elevator with us. He nodded once at Hunter, hit a button for his floor, and looked at me. His eyebrows rose above his glasses, giving away his shock before he spoke. "Mrs. Moriarty?"

I smiled, despite the frown that wanted to occur since I didn't recognize him. "Yes?"

"I'm surprised you're not with your husband at the hotel across town," he said.

Ah, he was mafia.

"I'm not attending that event," I explained with a wider, true smile. "Wives aren't really allowed there."

He smiled and held out his hand. "I'm Arturo Yaconelli. Nice to meet you."

The Yaconelli's were a powerful mafia, comprised of many different types of businesses. They rivaled us in terms of income, but had a much smaller territory located in the adjoining state.

I shook his hand and felt Hunter move closer to me. "It's nice to meet you as well. Are you staying at this hotel?" I knew he wasn't, but was trying to bait him into giving away why he was here when he very much should not have been.

He shook his head as he let go of my hand. "No, just playing the slots a bit before it's time to meet up. A friend is staying here, and I wanted to say hello to him as well."

For some reason the knowledge that he had a friend here made the hair on my nape stand on end. Who was his friend? Was it another mafia member? A spy that was part of Erina's family?

"Oh? Do I know them?" I asked, trying to play coy and cool.

He chuckled. "I doubt it."

The elevator opened on his floor and he bowed. "Have a good evening, Mrs. Moriarty. I hope we meet again."

"Likewise," I called as he left.

As soon as the doors closed, Hunter said, "He's suspicious."

I scoffed. "Thank you, Sherlock."

"It makes no sense for him to be here. It's almost a breech of the agreement for him to be in this hotel right now." Hunter's eyes narrowed. "I'm going to tell Shea."

I grabbed his arm as he reached for his phone. "No! If you tell Shea that Yaconelli is here, he's going to tell me that I have to leave. Just let it be. I'll tell Erina and she'll make sure the security team keeps an eye on him to ensure he leaves.

And, they'll keep an eye on whoever he is visiting. Do *not* tell any of my husbands! That is a direct order!"

He scowled, but nodded once. "Fine, but if something does happen, I get to rat you out afterwards."

I smiled and released his arm. "Deal."

Erina opened the door when we finally arrived, a scowl on her face. "You are late!"

I threw my arms around her and squealed. "Eri! I missed you! You're so pretty! Did you get work done? How come you look so much more beautiful? You're so much more beautiful than me now. How can I even stand next to such beauty? Is it allowed?"

She patted my back. "Flattery only gets you so far, Amelia."

I pointed at the bag that Hunter carried in. "I brought good champagne!"

"That will definitely earn you some points back!" Marlee said as she emerged from the bathroom to embrace me.

Once she released me, I fully walked into the hotel penthouse suite. The suite was located on the top floor of the hotel, offering stunning views of the city skyline from the floor-to-ceiling windows. The living room was spacious and elegantly furnished, with plush sofas and armchairs arranged around a coffee table. A large flat-screen TV was mounted on the wall, and a sleek sound system was built into the ceiling, providing the perfect backdrop for entertaining or relaxing. The dining area was equally impressive, with a long wooden table and high-backed chairs that could easily seat ten people. A crystal chandelier hung overhead, casting a warm and inviting glow over the entire room. The kitchen was fully equipped with high-end appliances, including a state-of-the-art oven and a large refrigerator. The marble countertops and sleek cabinetry added to the luxurious feel of the space. As I made my way to the bedrooms, I noticed the attention to detail and the quality of the furnishings. The master suite was particularly impressive, with a king-size bed outfitted with plush linens and pillows. The ensuite bathroom was spacious and beautiful, with a deep soaking tub and a separate walk-in shower. Erina already had her toiletry kit hanging next to the sink and a plush robe on the edge of the tub.

The second and third bedrooms in the suite were equally luxurious, with queen-size beds and private bathrooms. Each room had its own unique I and style, adding to the overall ambiance of the suite. As I stepped out onto the private balcony, I was greeted by a breathtaking view of the city skyline. The balcony was outfitted with comfortable lounge chairs and a small table, making it the perfect spot to relax and take in the view. Overall, the penthouse suite was a luxurious and unforgettable experience, offering the perfect blend of comfort, style, and elegance.

"What a view," Hunter commented beside me.

I turned and smiled at him. "You haven't stayed in a penthouse before, have you?"

He shook his head. "Nope, this is my first time."

"Well, get used to it," I said, patting his arm. "Only the best for you from now on."

"We need to start getting ready for dinner," Erina informed us as we walked back into the living room.

"Which room is mine?" Hunter asked.

"Two doors down," Erina told him. "Marlee's guard is the first room and the next is yours."

Hunter set my bag down and narrowed his eyes at me. "Do not leave this room until I return. Understand?"

I narrowed my eyes back at him and put my hands on my hips. "Who is the boss here?"

He pointed his finger at my face. "Do *not* leave this room until I return."

I stuck my tongue out at him as he left to get changed.

"He's a good addition to your harem," Erina said.

I rolled my eyes. She knew very well that he wasn't part of my group. "He's a pain in the butt, but does his job well." I clapped my hands together. "Let's have a pregame drink!"

Without waiting for her answer, I opened my bag, took out the champagne, and tried to open it.

Sadly, I sucked at it, but Marlee was a pro. She took it and opened it for us, not even letting the champagne fizz over at all as she poured it into glasses for us.

We clinked the edges of the glasses against each other and yelled, "Cheers!"

After a big sip, we all sighed and smiled simultaneously.

"To a wonderful weekend of fun and laughter," Erina said.

"Fun and laughter!" Marlee and I repeated and clinked our glasses against each other's again. This time, we drained our glasses and then set them on the counter.

"Let's hurry and get ready so we can get to dinner on time," Marlee said. "I haven't eaten and that champagne is going to hit my system fast!"

"Ditto!" Erina and I said in chorus.

With laughs, we split up to our respective rooms in the huge suite to change.

The dresses she'd chosen were absolutely gorgeous, and I made sure to style my hair and do my makeup before slipping mine on, not wanting to risk getting the makeup onto the dress as I did it. I was known for getting eyeshadow powder on my tops.

Once ready, we met in the living room area to take pictures and posed a ton of different ways before agreeing upon a single photo that we could post online.

I opened the door and Hunter smiled. "You look lovely."

"Thank you," I said and curtsied.

Erina and Marlee came out, letting the door shut behind them.

"You both look lovely as well," Hunter said.

Erina flipped her hair over her shoulder. "We know."

Hunter's smile spread at her response, knowing she was just teasing.

Two guards down the hallway stepped out ahead of us, pushing the button for the elevator.

"Oh, we each get our own guard this trip?" I asked.

Erina sighed. "Yeah, it was something our husbands apparently negotiated with each other."

"And yet Connor forgot you were even going today, didn't he?" I smiled wide, knowing I was right about her grumpy husband.

She laughed and shook her head. "That's why he plans ahead, because otherwise, it'll get forgotten."

"Sounds like Amelia," Hunter mumbled.

I spun and smacked his arm, though not hard. "You're being a terrible shadow right now!"

He straightened, wiped the smile off his face, and glared at the elevator doors. "Sorry, ma'am."

I nodded once, satisfied with the change in attitude, though I knew as soon as I turned away from him, he would relax again. In public was the only time he had to remain stoic as my guard. Any other time and he was free to just be himself.

"He better not distract you all night," Erina said, scowling at him and tapping her fingers against her crossed arms.

"He won't," I promised. "Once we get to the restaurant, he'll blend in and we won't even notice him."

"Okay," she said, but didn't seem convinced.

The restaurant hostess nearly tripped over her own feet in her hurry to take us to our table. They assigned us two waiters, making sure we didn't wait more than two minutes for our drinks and appetizers.

"To reunited friends!" I said as I raised my glass into the middle of the table.

Erina and Marlee clinked their glasses against mine and repeated what I'd said.

"So, did your husbands try to talk you out of going?" Marlee asked.

I rolled my eyes. "Do you even need to ask?"

Marlee and Erina laughed.

"They didn't try too hard, though. And I almost forgot my dress, but Stephan grabbed it for me." He was always reminding me about things I'd forgotten lately.

"I'm glad they're letting you do more without them now," Marlee said.

"Only because I have Hunter," I argued. "Pretty sure if I hadn't hired him that I'd have Dane with me right now."

"I wouldn't mind Dane. Shea is the one who draws all the attention," Erina said.

"It's not his fault he's so big," I said with a chuckle. The giant man did often draw attention just due to his size.

"That's what she said!" Erina shot back, making us all break out into laughter.

We took our time eating the food and drinking a few more drinks, not wanting to leave quickly.

"Do you think we should eat dessert here or go to our usual dessert place?" Erina asked.

"Both? Why not both?" I asked with wide, eager eyes, and a vigorous nod.

Marlee said, "I agree. Both."

"Let's split something here between the three of us and then by the time we get into the next place and order, we'll have more room for dessert!"

Erina laughed at my excitement. "You'd think that you aren't allowed sweets by the way you act, but we all know that you are spoiled and get sweets delivered and made for you all the time."

"Not all the time," I countered. "And honestly, I'm usually the one who makes it. So, it's a really nice treat to be somewhere where I don't have to make it myself."

"You say that, but as soon as you eat it, you're going to think of ways that you could improve it yourself at home," Marlee said, calling me out.

"You're not wrong," I mumbled and drained the last of my drink.

Erina raised her hand and the two waiters rushed over. "One chocolate lava cake to split."

"Yes, ma'am," they said and both zipped off to place the order.

"I need to open a restaurant, so I can get them to treat me that way." Glancing out of the corner of my eye, I spotted Hunter sitting at a table, sipping on a beer with an empty plate before him. He'd probably eaten steak, that was his favorite.

It was good to see him relaxing more. Since he'd taken the job as my bodyguard, he'd been stiff and on edge. Thankfully, nothing had happened recently, which meant he'd started to relax more.

Hunter had also relaxed more around the guys, opening up, and allowing us to really get to know him. We had quickly become friends, and while I had no romantic interest in him, I did consider him part of the family. Like a long lost brother I'd only found out about recently, but that fit incredibly well into our lives.

"How are the babies?" Marlee asked.

"Getting bigger and into mischief constantly!" I complained, though with a smile on my face. It was impossible to stay angry at the adorable girl and boy I helped create. Their unshakable love and trust was something I did not take lightly. Did that mean I was spooling them? Most likely. Was I the only parent doing it? Nope. "They've learned several signs now and it's really helping us communicate with them." Arcadio knew a little sign language and watched a ton of videos to learn which ones were the easiest for babies to learn and helped the most with communication before they could speak. It was honestly a lifesaver and prevented a lot of meltdowns from Callen when he couldn't get us to understand what he wanted.

"Is Callen still behind on speaking?" Erina asked, her voice softer.

I nodded. "He's saying a few words, but not as much as Paige, but he is signing more than Paige now. The doctors keep telling us not to worry, but..."

"But you're his mom, so of course you're going to worry," Erina finished.

"I'm sure everything will work out. Everyone learns at different paces," Marlee said. "Brian was actually a late speaker and now he can debate with the best of them."

That actually made me feel a lot better to hear her say that.

Marlee's eyes lit up when she saw the waiter carrying our cake. "Chocolate cake!"

"We should go to the spa tomorrow morning," I suggested as I picked up my fork, eyes focused on the plate the waiter carried, ready to absolutely devour the chocolate cake and scoop of vanilla ice cream atop it.

"Facials?" Erina asked.

"Massages," I countered. My neck muscles were sore from spending so much time playing videogames lately.

"Facials, massages, and manicures!" Marlee countered my counter.

"Can I do some gambling tonight?" I asked. Erina never

let me gamble and the guys never took me to casinos, but I'd always wanted to try it.

"Oh, I didn't tell you?" she asked with a scowl. "I swore I told you."

"Postpartum brain," I said with a knowing smile.

"We're going to have dessert now, then go gamble, drink, and then go to next dessert. I scheduled it with the guards already. I know you keep bugging me about trying your hand at roulette."

"I'm going to be amazing at it and win so much money! Just you wait!" I told her confidently.

"Like you need any more money," Marlee scoffed.

"I still like to make money on my own," I reminded her.

"Speaking of that. How's your mirror doing?" Erina asked.

Marlee looked over, obviously interested to hear, too.

"Really well, but I need to find something new to get out there, aside from the second edition of the mirror." I'd been racking my brain for months, trying to come up with a new invention. "I have several ideas and even a few prototypes, but nothing that I think is good enough to launch or good enough for our name. I've had so many focus groups review things and ultimately their hesitations were the same as mine, so I canned them all. Stephan said it's normal for inventors to have dozens of inventions that never see the light of day, but I'm beyond frustrated at not finding something at this point."

"I love how much interest you are taking in the business and the *business* now," Marlee said, and set her hand on top of mine on the table. "You're finally officially one of us."

"Do I get a membership card? Or a welcome basket?" I asked.

"Sure, I'll get you a welcome basket," she said and funny enough, I knew she wasn't joking. She totally would get me one.

"No fruit, please. I'm allergic."

Erina shook her head. "Allergic to healthy foods?"

"You sound like Forrest," I grumbled.

"That's because you need to eat better," Marlee said sternly. "You have been eating a lot of carbs instead of protein."

"Is this an intervention?" I asked, looked around us, and looked back at them. "Are my husbands going to pop out and join us to berate me and my eating habits? How do you even know what I've been eating?"

Hunter started to stand, seeing me look around. I waved my hand at him dismissively, and he sat back down.

"We're just saying that even on the calls we have with you, you have admitted that you aren't eating much protein and you know that protein is important," Marlee said.

"Fine. I'll eat more meat," I swore. "It's not like I don't like meat. It's just time consuming to defrost and cook."

"You are a billionaire. Hire a chef," Marlee said and rolled her eyes.

"We don't even have maids," I reminded her. "I'm not about to let a chef in who could poison me or my husbands." There was no way that I was going to give anyone the chance to harm me or mine by allowing them into my house to cook for us and poison us. "We've been better about setting up rotations on cooking," I explained. "Now that I'm more involved in... everything... they're taking it seriously and making sure that I'm not the only one handling meals and things like that. You don't need to worry so much."

They both looked at me skeptically, but I could see the understanding in Erina's eyes. She had a long time butler, someone she had known since she was young, so it was different for her.

"Maybe I'll just send Hunter to cooking school and make him our chef," I said with a wide smile.

That had both Erin and Marlee laughing and shaking their heads.

Chapter 5

Marlee

After finishing our first dessert, we headed to the gambling floor to mainly watch Amelia gamble. Gambling wasn't fun to me, but I knew watching Amelia for her first time gambling would be hilarious. Most things that woman did were hilarious.

"Fifty dollars says she pouts at her first loss," Erina whispered in my ear.

I rolled my eyes. "That's a guaranteed loss for me!"

We both chuckled, which had Amelia turning around to look back at us. She walked ahead, determined to find a roulette table that felt "good" to her.

Erina waved her hand. "Hurry and find a table before all the spots are taken."

Amelia's eyes narrowed, but she turned back around and did as she was told.

Finally, she found a table that had two open spots. There were a few older men in suits sitting in chairs with drinks and cigars, a couple men who were younger than us and obviously drunk, sloshing their half empty drinks around, and a few women around the older men who seemed to be escorts or trying to earn some quick cash from them. I was betting on those women making more money tonight than anyone else at the table.

Amelia took the spot next to the two younger guys and high-fived them for good luck.

I shook my head and laughed softly at her silliness, which never stopped making me smile.

"Are you sure you don't want our help with your problems?" Erina asked softly as we found a spot near Amelia, but out of the way of others. There were a lot of people around, but they wisely gave us space. It also helped that the guards, including Hunter, had made a triangle of angry presence around us.

I sighed and rubbed my forehead. "I don't know any more, E. Things are escalating and the craziness seems to never stop." My eyes found the bar nearby and I waved at Hunter.

He walked over. "Yes?"

"Can you get Erina, Amelia, and I drinks?" I requested.

"Margaritas?" he guessed.

I smiled and nodded. "Yes, thank you, Hunter."

He looked at Amelia at the table, back at the bar that was about one hundred feet away, and asked, "Can I send one of the other guards instead?"

Erina smirked. "You've grown fond of her, haven't you?"

Hunter's cheeks reddened and he looked down. "She's magnetic in a fun way I haven't experienced before. She's like..."

"Your long lost sister?" I guessed.

He looked up, eyes wide. "Yeah. Exactly."

Erina and I laughed.

"We feel the same. Yes, go ahead and send one of the others, instead, so you can stay close," I said. The last thing I wanted was for Amelia to get attacked and get blamed for sending Hunter away.

"Thank you." He nodded once, turned, and walked over to one of the guards, giving them the order.

"If you need anything from me, a place to sleep for a night, extra guards, an unregistered gun, a burial site for a body with no explanation, just let me know. I'm here for you," Erina whispered as she moved close enough for our arms to touch.

"I know and I appreciate you." I also knew that Amelia would give us any security tech we wanted, but that's not what we needed.

We needed more intel and spies than we currently had, to try to find the culprit, the bastard, responsible for all of the chaos we were currently experiencing.

I sneezed for the third time. The smoke in the casinos always made me sneeze and gave me a headache.

A group of younger guys, likely mid-twenties, cheered and high-fived each other when one of their members won.

"Come on red!" Amelia yelled.

The older men around her stared in bewilderment. Yeah, she was a bit bewildering when you first met her.

"Red. Red. Red," she chanted, her hands in fists and pumping each time she said the word.

I remembered the first time I met her. I'd thought she was

like an overexcited puppy, but it had truthfully endeared her to me. It was hard to find people who could still smile so easily in this lifestyle.

"Those old men are going to leave the table pretty quick with her being so loud," Erina said with a proud smile.

"Yes!" Amelia cheered when the ball went into a red number.

"Could you shut up?" An older man on the opposite end of the table snapped as he stood, setting down his cigar angrily into one of the cupholders.

Erina snapped her fingers and one of her guards immediately went over and set a hand on the old man's shoulder. "It's time for you to leave, sir."

"Wh-What?" He stammered as he was led away.

Amelia stuck her tongue out at his back before turning back around and placing more chips down to increase her bet, shaking her butt in excitement as she did.

"You ever wonder how someone who has gone through so much can be so chipper?" I asked. "She was kidnapped, shot, and who knows what else they won't tell us. Yet, she is constantly smiling and doing everything she can for others. It's inspirational."

Erina smiled softly. "She's something, alright. I think it comes from her mother. She's also a very upbeat person who went through a lot of adversity. What worries me is when she stops having adversities."

I looked at Erina with a raised eyebrow. "What do you mean?"

"Those of us who are used to things going wrong, what happens when things start going right? We don't believe it or we sabotage ourselves. I'm worried she may end up sabotaging herself."

That was true. I had seen and done some self-sabotage myself. Thankfully, my husband was a patient man and we had worked things out. Her husbands were patient as well, but if we could prevent that from happening at all, that would be the best possible solution.

"Well, good thing she has us," I said. "We'll help her and talk her out of whatever self-sabotage she schemes up."

Erina chuckled. "When has anyone ever talked her out of anything?"

That had us both laughing.

Amelia squealed and clapped her hands as she won again.

Erina bumped her shoulder against mine. "Thanks for coming."

"Thanks for inviting me," I said. "It's nice to be out and have some fun. I missed you guys."

"Sorry for being on lockdown," she said and flinched. "Connor was being a bit cantankerous."

"Is he ever not cantankerous?" I teased.

She laughed and shook her head, but the smile on her face showed the love she felt for him. "True. He is a crotchety bastard often."

"And you love him for it."

"I do," she agreed.

It was nice having friends who also had good relationships with their spouses. I'd met a few mafia wives who were miserable and didn't hide it. They almost seemed to despise their husbands, but still stayed with them. Brian was overbearing at times, but he loved me and we were best friends. At night, if his business took him longer to handle and I got into bed first, he would bring a glass of water to my night table, kiss my cheek, and make sure my covers were all the way up before going back to finish things. He also made sure to spend time with me doing things I enjoyed even if he didn't particularly like it, because he said he liked seeing me happy.

I, of course, did the same, but not everyone had that.

I was worried these mansion raids would end with him getting hurt and wanted to get to the bottom of it sooner than later. Part of me wanted to ask Amelia and Erina for help; they would immediately, but I also didn't want to get them involved unless necessary. There was also a sense of pride, needing to handle our own shit without outside help. Part of it was also my age. I was ten years older than Amelia, though I didn't feel like it when we were together, but I also had a lot more experience with the mafia side of things. I didn't want to admit to needing help from a younger, less experienced woman.

I was a stubborn and prideful woman, which I hoped wouldn't be my downfall.

Amelia cheered as she won again, pulling me from my mind, and made me smile.

Chapter 6

Amelia

"Stop smiling so smugly," Erina ordered me.

I waved the stack of cash in my hand at her. "You would be gloating too if you had won two thousand dollars on roulette."

"I still think you cheated," Erina said. "I'm going to have them watch the security footage."

I stuck my tongue out at her. "You're just jelly."

"So, are you going to buy our drinks since you have so much money now?" Marlee asked.

"I suppose it is the least I could do since you had to stand and watch me play for half an hour. And since Erina had that rude man thrown out."

"I don't know what you're talking about," she lied.

"You love me so much that when a man yelled at me, you had him tossed out of the casino. You l-l-love me."

She smiled. "Just a little. Besides, that type of behavior was uncalled for. He could have nicely asked you to quiet down or just gone to a different table. It's not like you're the first or last person who is loud when they're winning and gambling in general."

We went to one of the many bars in the casino, this one giving us a great view of the rest of the casino. It gave us a good vantage point should any craziness happen and still had great drinks. Plus, I got to people watch!

"Oh, I forgot to tell you earlier. Yaconelli was here and said he was visiting a friend. You should have your team look out for whoever he met with," I told Erina.

Her eyes widened and her mouth dropped open. "Yaconelli was inside of this hotel? And you didn't tell me!"

I flinched. "I got excited to see you and forgot. But yes."

She raised her hand and one of the guards rushed over. She gave him instructions and he immediately pulled out his phone and called someone, stepping away from us so we wouldn't have to listen to his conversation.

"That bastard knows he's not supposed to come in here," she growled. "Connor is going to be pissed."

"Are you sure we have to tell them right away?" I winced. "My husbands are likely to rush over if they know one of the other mafia bosses is here."

"Ma'am," the guard said, interrupting us. "He's left the casino and gone to the meeting."

"His friend?" Erina asked.

"He's gambling and we are looking into his identity now. I'll let you know as soon as we find out."

She nodded and waved her hand. "Thank you."

Hunter spoke with the two other guards, relaxed a bit, and retook his spot in a chair in the front corner of the bar area.

"What drinks do you want this time?" I asked. "More margaritas or bubbly to celebrate my win?"

"You choose, since you're paying," Marlee said. "Though, if we don't want awful hangovers tomorrow, it might be better to stick to one type of drink."

Instead of being demanding like Erina would, I stood and went to the bar top, sliding in between two seats where the men in them were sipping bourbons on ice.

The bartender hurried over, wide-eyed. "Yes, ma'am? What can I get for you?"

"Three glasses and a bottle of your best champagne," I ordered.

"Right away, I'll have someone bring it out to you, so you don't need to wait up here," he said and reached into one of the small fridges under the bar.

"Thank you," I replied, chipper, and spun around on my heel.

"Look at these spoiled rich bitches," one of the men beside me said and scoffed. "Out here spending their husbands' money like it's fake. Never thought to even get a job of their own."

Normally, I would have ignored his comment, knowing we weren't like that, but the few drinks I'd had changed that reaction. I spun right back around on my heel so I could face him. Smiling wide, I held out my hand. "Hello, sir. I don't think we've met. I'm Amelia Moriarty."

His eyes widened and his mouth dropped, but he still shook my hand. He wore a suit with the tie loosened and a few buttons opened. Clearly, he wasn't having a good night. "Mrs. M-Moriarty. I didn't recognize you."

"How could you when I'm dressed up like a gold digger today instead of my usual self." I leaned closer to him and whispered, "You might get laid if you weren't so judgmental. I mean your statement was just a long-winded way to say you're not getting any. Might rethink that in the future."

I patted his back and skipped over to our table, taking my seat again, and crossed my legs since I wore a dress.

"What did you do?" Erina asked.

"Introduced myself," I said and shrugged.

"He went from angry to shocked to immediately leaving," Marlee said and laughed. "You definitely didn't just introduce yourself."

"Well, he was being mean so I told him that he basically just told us he wasn't getting laid without telling us he wasn't getting laid." I shrugged.

Erina and Marlee burst out laughing.

The bartender brought out a small silver tub with ice and a bottle of champagne, as well as the three glasses I had requested. After doing a toast and cheers, I looked around the casino for some people watching. My eyes caught on someone that looked familiar, but it couldn't be him ... could it?

It looked like ... Angel Eyes.

"Amelia?" Marlee asked.

I stood, trying to get a better look, but the man was gone, disappearing within the crowds. I sat back down and shook my head. "Sorry, thought I saw someone."

"We get it, you're super popular," Erina said with extreme side eye.

Rolling my eyes, I shook my head. "Whatever, you are haters."

Drinking more of the tasty beverage, I refocused on my friends. Angel Eyes wasn't here. I was just being paranoid now.

A group of twenty-something men stumbled towards the bar area, laughing and teasing each other. They noticed us and veered our way.

"Hello, ladies," one of them greeted with an overexaggerated tone, swaying slightly.

"Keep moving," Hunter ordered them, coming up to my side immediately.

"Who are you?" one of the men asked, looking down his nose at Hunter.

"He said, 'keep moving' and you should listen," one of Erina's guards ordered them, the second one coming up behind him.

The young men's eyes widened and the one who'd greeted us held up his hands and backed towards the bar. "Sorry, we're going."

"Thank you," I said softly to Hunter.

He nodded once and he and the other two returned to their seat at the table beside us.

The young men took seats at the bar, but I noticed they kept looking at us.

"Maybe we should move after we finish these drinks," I suggested as I took another sip.

"I'm not letting some young bucks force me to leave. They can go somewhere else or try my men," Erina said, relaxing more in her seat.

"Pretty sure Hunter is looking for a chance to hit some-one. He got here much faster than the other two," Marlee commented.

"My husbands gave him very specific and detailed instructions and threatened him a lot to keep me safe," I explained. "He's just doing his job."

"He cares about you, you know?" Marlee whispered.

I nodded. "We're friends. Well, more like siblings now. We play games together all the time."

"I'm glad you have someone you can trust. I know how untrusting you lot are," Erina said.

I mimicked her. "Whatever."

"Untrusting and yet they got together pretty quickly," Marlee muttered.

"Actually, they ran background checks on me before we officially started dating," I explained. It wasn't really a secret, but I wasn't sure I was supposed to tell them. My husbands likely wouldn't care.

"Oh my god! Connor did that, too!" Erina said and shook her head. "I was pissed when I found out."

I shrugged. "It made sense to me."

"Of course it did." Marlee shook her head with a smirk. "I'm surprised you didn't run background checks on us before becoming our friends."

I gave her a huge smile and said, "I didn't need to because Stephan already had."

We stared at each other in silence a moment before all three of us burst into laughter. Clearly, they had expected that answer.

One of Erina's guards got a phone call and stepped away to take it.

"How did you and Brian meet?" I asked, since I'd never heard about it and was curious.

"We met in school, college, actually," Marlee answered. "We were part of the same group project and, as with most projects, our other members sucked. We ended up spending several late nights together, working on the project and getting to know each other. He asked me out on a date one day and we've pretty much been inseparable ever since."

"Aw," I squealed.

She shook her head and laughed.

Erina's guard returned and stood stiffly by Hunter. Obviously, whatever that phone call had been, he hadn't liked it.

Marlee and Erina ordered another round and we sat in a bit of silence, people watching and enjoying each other's company.

Normally, I would have started another conversation, but I didn't want to ruin the current, quiet, happiness.

Another group tried to get close to us and Hunter stepped up immediately, getting them to leave.

Erina's two guards stayed on the wall. They looked like statues almost. While it was nice having a guard, I was glad I had someone like Hunter with a personality. I would go insane with guards like hers. They were so tense. So quiet. Just... staring. It seemed like one was staring at Marlee more than Erina, but maybe it was just my viewpoint.

Yet again, another guy tried to approach our table. I sighed and shooed him with my hands. "Leave us alone."

He leaned over and said, "I bet I could buy you ladies a round of drinks."

"No thanks, we're good," Erina said.

The man didn't take the hint, his slurred words more pronounced now. "Come on, just one round."

I raised my hand and Hunter, hurried over. "There a problem?" he asked.

"No problem, man. Just offering these beautiful women a drink," the guy said and swayed slightly on his feet.

"They're not interested," Hunter said sternly. "And you don't seem to know when to take no for an answer. I think it's time for you to leave the bar."

"Psh, you don't get to tell me what to do, bub!" the man said, shoving his finger into Hunter's chest.

Hunter smiled and there was nothing nice about it. Two seconds later, the guy had a broken finger and his arm shoved up behind his back as Hunter lead him over to one of the security guys who happened to be passing by.

"Some men just can't take a hint," I said and shook my head.

Erina's guards remained statues on the wall, no longer coming to help when men bothered us. Was it because Hunter was so quick to approach? Or was it something else?

Chapter 7

Marlee

People watching had always been one of my favorite things to do. As a wife to a mafia boss, I was often overlooked, seen as a decoration instead of a knowledgeable, intelligent woman with several degrees and a history within mafias.

So, I kept to the back of the room, letting the idiotic people who underestimated me watch them, undisturbed, and learned more secrets than they would ever had been willing to part with.

Now, one of my favorite things was people watching with my girls.

"Oh, there," Amelia said and jerked her chin towards a couple walking through the entrance.

The man was well in his eighties, a black cane with a silver tip in his hand, and a woman in a mini skirt and stilettos on his arm. She laughed at something he said, gently setting her hand on his arm as she laughed exuberantly, her perfectly straight, white teeth flashing. As she bent slightly from the laugh, her cleavage became more exposed and he made no show of hiding his stare.

"If she doesn't get at least five thousand dollars out of that man tonight, I'd be surprised," Erina said.

"That one," I said and pointed towards a younger couple.

The man wore a pair of black slacks, a button up shirt with the sleeves rolled up but first few buttons undone to expose thick black chest hair, and had several tribal tattoos on his arms. The woman wore a lightweight black dress with a plunging neckline and her concealer a shade darker than the rest of her exposed skin. She looked uncomfortable, nervous, but kept smiling whenever he spoke to her.

"Newer couple, this is her first time at a casino," Amelia said.

"Yeah, too easy," Erina agreed.

"What about him? Family or no?" I asked.

"Oh," Amelia said, leaned forward with her elbows on her knees, and watch them a bit longer "I say no."

"I say yes," Erina said. "He's got that cocky walk that the newer, lower level mafia guys have. The ones who think that just because they're part of the mafia means they're in the big leagues even though they are only handling the easiest shit."

Oh, he did have that aura about him. I remembered noticing it on Brian when we'd first started hanging out more. Remembered how I'd wondered if he was really a good guy or a douche I should avoid as quickly as possible. I was glad I had not avoided him back then.

Six women wearing matching v-neck shirts with "Last Fling Before the Ring" on the back and black tulle skirts walked in with large glasses of margaritas. In the center of the group was a petite blonde haired woman with a tiara wearing a white satin dress with a sash over her chest that said "Bride To Be" with a necklace made of tiny neon colored plastic penises bouncing as she walked.

"That's something I actually never got," I commented softly.

"What?" Erina asked.

"A bachelorette party," I answered. "At that time, I didn't really have friends and it seemed like a silly thing to do anyway, so I didn't do one. Now, I realize it's just another excuse to get your friends together, drink, and celebrate."

"Do you want me to throw you a bachelorette party?" Amelia asked. "I could throw the *best* bachelorette party."

A bachelorette party thrown by Amelia would definitely be an event to see, but I was only slightly jealous of those women now.

"No, thank you. I do appreciate the offer, but we don't need a themed party when we can just get together like this and drink and hang out."

"True," she said with a nod. She stood and did a spin. "And look at the gorgeous dresses we're wearing. Way better than those tulle skirts."

"Exactly," I said with a nod and smoothed a hand down my dress.

"Well, that's because your friend has excellent taste in clothes," Erina said and brushed imaginary lint off her shoulder.

"That she does," I agreed with a nod.

"Oh, them," Amelia said, drawing our attention back to people watching.

A tall, handsome man in a grey pinstriped suit with a white handkerchief in his pocket walked into our area. He had shiny black shoes, a deep red tie, and a five o' clock shadow outlining his rugged jaw. His eyes were a deep crystalline blue and he had a perfect smile.

"Whoa," I whispered.

"Handsome, right?" Amelia said with a nod. "I don't get to admire the *scenery* as much as I used to, but whew that's a handsome man."

I supposed it would be hard to admire a handsome man when you had five around you. Not as easy to sneak a peek with that many eyes on you at once.

"You poor thing," I teased. "Unable to sneak a peek at a man due to have too many sexy ones sitting around you."

She smiled. "See, you do understand my dilemma."

"I actually do," Erina said. "Sometimes, I get caught and they act like I kissed the guy just because I watched him walk by a little too long." She sighed heavily. "I can't really fault them, though, because I do the same when I see them watch a woman walk by."

"The most fun is when you catch each other watching someone walk by," Amelia said with a soft laugh. "Then you just go, 'I know, right' and laugh it off."

We played our guessing, people watching game for a bit longer, but eventually relaxed to do the watching silently.

As I sipped on my newest drink, I couldn't help noticing one of Erina's guards continually glancing at me.

Was it me he was glancing at or was I just being paranoid? Erina was right next to me, so maybe it was just that he was looking in our direction to make sure no one was bothering us.

Taking a deep, cleansing breath, I tried to relax more. I was still definitely too wound up and frustrated with my recent experiences. Nothing was going to happen here, in this hotel, surrounded by mafia guards. I was safe and my girls were with me.

If anything, Amelia was probably the best protection I had. The insane, tiny tornado would shoot someone faster than I could voice the order.

That thought brought a smile to my face and finally, I relaxed a little bit more.

Chapter 8

Amelia

Something was off. I couldn't place it, but I could feel it. It was like the air had shifted and become thicker, tenser. Yet, there was no single event that I could place to have caused it.

When had the change in atmosphere happened?

Was it when Marlee's guard got the phone call, or before?

"What's wrong?" Erina asked, noticing my scowl as we walked down the hallway, heading towards our room.

I turned, mouth opened to respond, but quickly snapped it shut.

The guard who'd gotten the phone call grabbed Marlee, one large arm hooked around her chest and holding her against his body so she couldn't move. "No one move or I'll shoot you," he threatened, gun leveled at us.

Hunter backed up, moving closer to me, but kept his hands loose at his sides.

"What are you doing?" Erina demanded. "You work for me."

The guard sneered. "Yeah, but you don't pay as well as other players in town."

Other players in town. Not other players. Was that an important distinction?

"What do you want?" I asked calmly and took a few steps forward, closing the distance between him and us.

"Don't fucking move," he ordered me and pointed the gun at my face.

I raised my hands. "Bro, are you really intimidated by me?" I looked down at my peacock dress then back at him with an arched brow.

"She and I are going to leave and you lot are going to stay here," he said.

"I don't think so," Erina said and her hands clenched into fists at her side.

Erina's guard at least seemed to be good still and on our side. He stepped closer to her, his hands at his sides, ready to grab his gun when he could, and half of his body in front of Erina's in case the other idiot tried to shoot her.

My dagger was strapped to my thigh, but to use it before he pulled the trigger, I needed to be closer to him. I needed to be within striking distance.

"Don't do anything reckless," Hunter whispered behind me.

"Ready?" I asked instead of responding to his stupid statement.

He sighed. "Yeah."

"So, how much are they paying you, and who is paying you?" I asked, cocking a hand on my hip.

"Twice the guard fee and a bonus when I deliver her alive," he said with a wide smile.

"Well, that's really unfortunate," I said and shook my head, sliding my hand down my side towards my hip where the slit in my dress was and my concealed dagger.

"Unfortunate?" he asked.

I smiled. "Since you're going to die in this hallway." Jerking my dagger out of the sheath on my leg, I stabbed it into his thigh as I ducked down.

"Ow!" he yelled, pointing the gun towards me.

Hunter darted forward, his arms wrapped around the man's legs, and he tackled him away from Marlee and I.

Immediately, Hunter used his MMA experience to get the better position and within a few seconds had the larger man pinned on the ground with his arm behind his back.

"Orders?" Hunter asked.

"Kill him," Erina barked.

Hunter drew his gun and shot the man in the back of the head immediately, zero hesitation.

Erina pulled out her phone and called someone. "Cleanup. My current location."

"Are you okay?" I asked Marlee as I straightened and set my hands on her arms.

She threw her arms around me and buried her face in my hair. "Thank you."

I patted her back and smiled. "That's what friends are for."

"Why Marlee?" Erina asked as she scowled down at the dead man.

What did it say about me and my friends that we could care less that there was a dead body beside us?

"I don't know," I admitted and realized that perhaps we should have questioned him a bit more before killing him, but it was a little late for that now. I wasn't too upset about it, though. I'd rather Marlee be safe than have more information and her injured.

"You okay?" Hunter asked me.

I raised a brow. "Pretty sure that's my line. You're the one who tackled and subdued him and then shot him."

"I would have killed him sooner, but wasn't sure you wanted him dead," he admitted.

I patted his arm. "You did great. Ten out of ten job. Would totally recommend."

He rolled his eyes at me and I wondered if he realized how often he did it? Would he develop issues with his eyes from rolling them so much or would they become stronger from the excess workouts he was doing with them?

A group of men in suits rounded the corner, two carrying a gurney, and one a black bag. The cleanup crew had arrived.

"Medical attention needed?" one of the men asked.

Erina shook her head. "No, but I want his phone unlocked and access to his messages."

He nodded bent down, searched through the dead man's pockets, and once he had the phone, pressed the dead man's thumb to the screen. It unlocked and he immediately handed it to Erina.

Why hadn't I thought of that? I turned to Hunter and said, "Next time, make sure you do what he just did after killing a guy, okay? You know I'll forget."

He smirked. "Okay."

She scrolled through the messages and waved at us to follow her towards the elevator. "Let's go up to the room to review this in private."

Hunter walked at my side. "Should I call—"

I interrupted him immediately. "We aren't calling until we have all of the information. They're just going to bark at you to find out more, so it's best to wait."

Turning towards Marlee, I gave her a once over. She didn't look shaken up. Quite the contrary, she looked mad. "Are you okay?"

She nodded. "I'm just upset."

Erina stopped, spun around, and looked at Marlee with wide eyes. "I swear, I didn't know anything about this. I never would have—"

Marlee wrapped Erina in a hug. "I know, bitch. I'm not mad at you. I'm just mad that shit like this keeps happening. Once my overprotective husband finds out, I don't think he's going to let me leave the house for a year, if ever again."

"We'll just kidnap you," I promised with a wide smile and joined their hug.

Once in the hotel room, Hunter peered over Erina's shoulder to look at the phone. He wrote down some notes and started his own research.

Marlee and I poured more drinks, setting Erina's in front of her before we started drinking ours.

"I do have to say, trips with you girls are never boring," Marlee commented with a smirk.

"So kind of you to say," I replied and raised my glass in a salute.

"I had hoped this would be boring, but here we are," Erina grumbled. Her phone chimed and her eyes widened. "Well, I know who our culprit is."

"Please don't say Angel Eyes," I whispered over and over again in a chant-like prayer.

She nodded. "Angel Eyes."

I groaned and let my head fall back. "I said *not* to say that." Sitting upright, my eyes widened as I realized that I had seen him. "I thought I saw him walk by while we were sitting downstairs, but he disappeared into the crowd before I could be sure, so I assumed I was mistaken. Dammit, I should have known it would be him." Why was he so interested in me? Or, did it not have to do with me? I knew not everything was about me.

"Is he here for the meetings?" Marlee asked.

"Possibly," Hunter commented. "We know he's been expanding his territory and group." He looked at me. "You know we need to mention him to Stephan."

I cringed. "Do we?"

"He needs to know he's in the same town as you where you aren't as protected. That man made an offer for you."

Narrowing my eyes at Hunter I replied, "I remember."

"I'm calling," Hunter said, stood, and walked towards his room with his cell phone out.

I chugged my drink and stood to get another. "This is going to be an ugly phone conversation."

"Maybe we should retreat to my house?" Erina suggested. "It's the closest and safer than here."

I was just about to agree when Hunter returned, scowling down at his phone. "What's up?" I asked.

"No one is answering their phones. In fact, they're all turned off," he explained.

Turned off? They wouldn't have turned their phones off. And they definitely wouldn't have ignored our calls.

I grabbed my phone off the table and dialed Stephan. The call instantly went to voicemail. Dialing all of the others resulted in the same. This was not good. Something was going on and I wasn't sure what it was.

"Did you try the backup?" I asked. Stephan kept a discreet backup phone that didn't look like a phone on him at all times. It was for emergency situations.

He nodded. "Same thing."

Fuck.

"We need to get over there," I said and stood. "We need to find out what's going on at that meeting."

"What are you two talking about?" Marlee asked.

"Try calling your husbands," I ordered Marlee and Erina. "Mine go straight to voicemail, including the secret backup phone Stephan has."

Erina's eyes widened and she and Marlee quickly tried their husbands' phones.

As I had worried, they had the same outcome. All phones were turned off and went straight to voicemail.

I opened the tracking app on my phone, the one tied to the tracking devices that were hidden inside a piece of jewelry each of the guys wore. It showed them all in the same place not far from here. After cross referencing the location with a map, I confirmed it was the hotel they were supposed to have the meetings at.

"My guys are still at the hotel, so I think it's safe to

assume that no matter what's happened, we need to get to them. Are there guns in this room?" I asked Erina.

She shook her head. "No, but we can go downstairs and gear up."

I nodded. "I think that's a necessity."

"How many weapons do you have on you?" I asked Erina's guard.

"Two handguns and a taser," he answered immediately.

"We definitely need to gear up," I said with an increased sense of foreboding.

"Good thing we've sobered up," Marlee said and shook her head. "Right when I was about to make another drink, too."

"Same," I muttered. Whatever was going on, we were going to head over and find out. Even though we were going to gear up, I worried about taking too long to get over there. Who know what kind of trouble they were in?

Erina led us down the hallway to an employee only elevator. She hit the button for a floor labeled "A-1".

"What's that mean?" I asked.

"Armory," she answered automatically.

"Of course you have an armory here." I shook my head, but couldn't help smiling.

"Don't act like you don't have an armory under your building," she said, arching a brow.

"We have a weapons department since we develop weapons there," I reminded her.

"Super convenient excuse," she scoffed.

The doors opened and a giant man wearing a suit with a stoic expression blocked our way.

"Hello, Butch," Erina greeted.

He nodded once, expression unchanged. "Boss."

"My friends and I need to get some gear," she said. "Please step aside."

After looking us over, he pivoted to the side, revealing a door behind him. "Make sure you check them out."

She patted his arm. "Yes, yes. I'll follow the rules."

"First time for everything," he muttered as we passed by.

A bark of laughter escaped before I could stop it. "He's obviously dealt with you on more than one occasion."

Erina shook her head. "Yeah, there's a safe room down here that they've forced me to use more than once."

We stepped through the door and Hunter whistled. "That is a lot of weaponry."

"We don't have suits or anything to change into, but we can put any large weapons not concealable in a bag," she explained.

I saluted her. "Yes, boss!" Pivoting on my heel, I perused the weapons, choosing a handgun with a silencer and a shotgun.

Hunter took the shotgun from me and put it in the bag he had picked up.

"Grab lots of ammo," I ordered him. "We don't know what we're going to run up against."

He nodded and went over to the table with stacks of ammunition boxes to do as I instructed.

I was about to turn around when I spotted a shiny set of ninja stars. "Oh, yeah." I grabbed them, put them in the pocket-sized carrying case on the table next to them, and tucked them into my bra.

"Really?" Erina asked with a smile.

"Of course she found ninja stars that she can put in her bra," Marlee said, shaking her head while laughing.

"You should grab a dagger," I ordered her. "And give Hunter a larger weapon for you, too."

"I don't know how to shoot anything other than a handgun," she replied.

"Point at bad guy, pull trigger, bad guy dies," I explained.

Hunter held up a shotgun. "This is how you load it and chamber a round." He demonstrated.

"Just give her an automatic one," Erina said from across the room where she was writing something down on a piece of paper.

"You have automatic shotguns?" Hunter asked.

"Back left wall," she answered.

Hunter set down the shotgun he'd had in his hands and hurried over to the spot she'd indicated and grabbed two of those.

"I don't want an automatic one," I informed him.

"Okay," he said and put the two automatic shotguns into the bag.

"Anything else?" Erina asked.

"We're set," I said. I checked the handgun I held to make sure it was loaded and turned the safety on.

"We should go out a side entrance, just in case Angel Eyes has more people trying to get Marlee or us," I suggested.

Erina nodded. "Already planned on it."

We filed out of the room and Erina waved to Butch and her guard, ordering him to stay behind to try to fix things in the hotel and root out the ones who were traitors.

I tried the guys' cell phones again, but they all went to voicemail.

Dammit. If that bastard hurts one of my men, I will make his death super painful.

I knew Stephan and knew that he would do whatever he could to get him and the guys back home safe. What could Angel Eyes have planned? What was his goal? Did he think he could really kill them and get away with it? That I wouldn't retaliate?

He was stupid if that's what he thought.

"You've got your murder face on," Marlee commented.

I raised my head to meet her eyes and frowned. "My what?"

"When you're thinking about murdering someone you make a very distinct face," she answered.

Looking at Hunter, I asked, "Is she right?"

He smiled. "Yep."

"Well, that's good to know," I said. "I have to try to keep my face more neutral, so my enemies won't know I'm about to shoot them."

"Pretty sure the gun aimed at their face will tip them off," Marlee teased.

The elevator doors opened to the back hallway of the first floor of the casino. Two men in slacks and button-up shirts wearing golden nametags stood in the hallway. They both turned around, eyes widened, and raised their handguns towards us.

"Found them!" one of the men yelled over his shoulder.

Chapter 9

Marlee

Erina hit the button to close the doors and selected a different floor. The telltale sounds of bullets hitting the elevator doors echoed inside the elevators as we went up another floor.

"What the hell was that? Weren't those some of your employees?" I demanded.

"They must have been paid by Angel Eyes, too," Erina said with a sigh. "What is happening to this casino?"

"Where are we going?" Hunter asked.

"The next floor has an emergency exit right by the elevator. It's our best bet to get out if there are more of the hotel staff that are on his payroll now." She looked at Amelia and me and winced. "The exit is a firepole."

Amelia looked down at her dress with the high slit on one side. "You want me to go down a firepole in this dress?" she asked.

"It's the best option," she said.

"Put your handguns in the bag," Hunter ordered us. "I'll go down first to make sure it's clear."

"We'll be weaponless up here," Amelia argued, and I agreed. I didn't like the idea of being weaponless when they were shooting at all of us now.

"You can't slide down the pole with the gun," he argued back.

Amelia tilted her chin up and said, "Watch me."

I smiled, but turned so she couldn't see it. She was always so feisty and never backed down with her husbands or Hunter.

He sighed. "Fine, whatever. I'm still going down first."

"I'll go last," she said, "that way I can cover our backs."

Erina nodded. "Marlee goes after Hunter, since they seem to be after her."

"I don't know. Those gunshots just now didn't seem like they were trying to kidnap me," I countered.

"I think they were trying to kill Erina and Amelia," Hunter commented. "That's where their guns were aimed."

"Wonderful," Erina grumbled.

The elevator opened, Erina exited, turned to the right, and pushed a button on a light fixture. The wall to the right got a sudden split down part of it, which popped out. A hidden door. That was super cool and I wanted to add more things like that in our house. No, *needed*. I needed them. Super concealable doors would be great to have for quick escapes.

"Secret doors like that would be great for pulling pranks on my husbands," Amelia commented.

Moonlight streamed in and the sounds of cars, people, and city nightlife assaulted us. It was jarring to go from the quiet hotel with white noise machines to make it even quieter to the outside sounds. There was a small platform with a single metal pole attached to the building.

Hunter looked at Amelia with a scowl and said, "Don't dally."

"Stay safe," she ordered him.

He stepped out onto the small platform, gripped the pole, and slid down.

"He did that really well. You think he used to be a fireman?" Erina asked.

"More likely a pole dancer," I said.

Amelia laughed, turned to face the hallway in case anyone came after us, and flicked the gun safety off. "He does not have the dance skills to have been a stripper."

"Clear!" Hunter called up.

Anxiety built in my chest. I wasn't afraid of heights, but I did not want to slip or fall going down the pole. That would be a great headline: Mafia Wife Died Falling Off A Pole.

Amelia squeezed my hand. "We're right behind you."

I nodded, straightened my spine, and walked to the pole. "Don't look up my dress, Hunter."

"Yes, ma'am."

Erina and Amelia laughed.

I grabbed the pole, with one hand, took a deep breath, and wrapped my legs around it as I slid down.

Chapter 10

Amelia

The sound of the elevator ding announcing someone getting off on this floor made me turn. Two people exited the elevator, guns in their hands.

"Go," I ordered Erina.

"Amelia—"

"Go," I hissed.

She obeyed, thankfully.

The two people, men, turned towards us.

I raised my gun and said, "Don't move or I'll shoot."

They froze.

I backed up slowly towards the exit.

"Is that her?" a male voice asked from my right, down the open hallway.

"Shit." I was out of time. I hit the button on the light fixture, and stepped out onto the small platform. I mentally cursed whoever decided to make it so small.

The men raised their weapons. I fired, hitting the first guy just before the door shut.

Grabbing the pole, I slid down while still aiming up, just in case one of the guys managed to open the door.

My feet hit the ground and I almost fell, but Hunter righted me. "Thanks," I said and smiled at him.

He shook his head. "You're going to give me grey hairs."

I touched his temples. "Pretty sure you already have some."

He smacked my hand away gently. "Let's go."

"Do you know where we're going?" I asked, looking around at the alley we were in.

"I know you three are going to want to head straight to the hotel, so we can see what's happening with your husbands," Hunter answered.

"Correct," I said with a nod.

"It's a five block walk from here," Hunter added.

"Is there a vehicle we can take?" Marlee asked. "I don't really want to walk five blocks in these heels, while people are trying to kill us. Walking barefoot is even less appealing when you know how many people pee and defecate everywhere in this city."

"There are SUVs, but I'd have to get the keys and I'm not sure who I can trust anymore." Erina looked down, her brows furrowed, and a myriad of emotions visible.

It had to hurt to have people who you considered part of your family turn on you. Now I was worried about our group. Had they gotten to any of them? Was I going to have to look over my shoulder all of the time now? Were we going to have to investigate and possibly purge our people?

How deep did his infiltration run?

All that mattered was killing him. Once he died, things would be fine. We could handle all of the other details later.

"We could steal a car," I suggested.

"Yeah, let's do that," Erina agreed.

Hunter frowned. "I don't know how to hotwire a car. Do any of you?"

Marlee and Erina turned to me.

I sighed. "Yes, I know how."

"Let's hurry before they find their way out of the hotel to here," Erina urged.

We headed down the alley and out to one of the main streets, headed away from the casino.

Looking in each of the cars and searching for one I was certain I could hotwire ended up taking us two blocks. Luck was on our side since some poor idiot had left their keys in the car.

Hunter demanded to drive and I decided it wasn't a battle worth having and let him. We stopped half a block away from the hotel the meetings were happening in and waited.

There were no gunshots or explosions.

The front entry looked normal.

"Ready?" I asked.

"Nope," Marlee said softly.

I would have told her to stay in the car, but it was better to stay together, not split the party.

If Hunter would have done what I ordered him to do, I would have sent him off with Marlee back to our place.

He wouldn't let that happen, though.

"Just stay between us, okay? We're going to get upstairs, kill Angel Eyes, and rescue our husbands."

"How do you know they're even alive?" she asked, tears in her eyes.

"I don't," I admitted. "I just have hope. And Angel Eyes better have them alive or I'm going to kill him very, very, very slowly." I gave her my best smile. "Now, let's go save our men."

"I'll take point," Hunter said.

"I'll take rear," I volunteered.

He scowled.

"Of the three of us, I'm the best shot," I pointed out. "I'm much more used to gunfights than they are."

"She's right," Erina admitted. "She's got much better aim than me."

"I don't even like shooting guns," Marlee mumbled.

"Hopefully, you won't have to." I was going to do whatever I could to keep her safe.

"Alright, let's go!" I shouted cheerfully.

We exited the car and I put the keys between the sun visor and the roof. The guards out front didn't pay attention to us since we blended in with the rest of the nightlife, which worked in our favor as we headed around the side of the hotel, searching for a way in that wouldn't alert Angel Eyes' men. Luck was on our side as a couple of hotel employees stepped out an employee-only entrance to smoke.

Hunter caught the door before it closed and let us go in first.

"Hey, you can't go in there," one of the employees called

out, but Hunter simply closed the door behind us and took his spot as point again.

"Do you know which floor?" Erina asked as we found a service elevator nearby.

"Top floor," Hunter answered as he pushed the button to call the elevator. "They reserved the entire top floor."

We climbed in and I made sure I was in the front, next to Hunter.

"Marlee, stay behind me when the elevator doors open. Erina, you stay behind Hunter. They'll likely fire at us once we step out, so we'll also have to start shooting and hopefully, be able to move behind cover."

"You sure are bossy," Erina teased.

"She really is. No wonder you're not allowed to go with them on more gunfights," Marlee added.

"Following my directions will keep you alive," I said smugly. I reached into the duffle bag Hunter held loosely between us, pulled out the automatic shotgun and handed it to Marlee, then pulled out the shotgun I'd chosen and slung it over my shoulder. "We need to get more shotguns with straps," I commented to Hunter. "These are really helpful."

"Don't get shot," he ordered me.

"Now who's being bossy?" I teased.

We finally arrived to the top floor and I took a deep, steadying breath and switched off the safety on the handgun.

Chapter 11

Amelia

My expectations were not met as the doors opened to an empty hallway.

Hunter and I stepped out, looking each way, but there was no one visible.

I took out the tracking app and sighed. "It's not accurate enough to tell where they are."

Hunter looked over my shoulder, hit a few buttons, and the app interface changed, giving me more of a direct location. "You think Stephan wouldn't have the best tracking app possible for his wife, who was voted most likely to get kidnapped?"

Erina and Marlee snickered behind us.

Turning in a slow circle to test the app, I faced the direction my guys were in and pointed. "This way."

"Give me the phone," Marlee ordered me. "I'll give directions while you keep your hands available to shoot people."

"Good idea," I said as I handed her the phone and resumed walking.

At the next turn, Hunter poked his head out, then darted back. He held up two fingers.

I nodded, and whispered to the girls, "Stay here. Erina watch our backs."

She turned to face the opposite way, handgun at the ready.

Hunter counted down from three with his fingers and we both stepped out, weapons raised as we did. The two men opened their mouths, but didn't have time to raise their weapons before we shot them.

We stayed still, guns still raised, and waited in case anyone else was down that way or would come out after hearing the shots. Even with a silencer, the pop of the guns was loud.

"Point," Erina snapped behind us and shot her gun.

Hunter and I spun around.

Five men in suits with sunglasses on entered at the end of the hallway, headed our way. Erina's shot went wide, missing the men, but making them pause and draw their weapons.

Hunter and I moved forward, getting in front of Marlee and Erina, all while shooting at the men.

Some ducked around the corner and started taking shots from their hidden places.

"Get around the corner," I ordered everyone and started backing up.

Hunter and I took down three of the men, but there were still two more taking shots at us around the corner.

Just as we made it around the corner, one of the shots grazed Hunter's arm, making him drop the bag. Thankfully, he had dropped it around the corner, so I didn't need to reach into the open to get it.

He hissed in pain and I immediately grabbed bandages from the bag.

"Didn't I tell you *not* to get shot?" I grumbled.

"Well, it's not the first time I've disobeyed your orders," he said with a chuckle. "And it's just a graze."

"Blood loss is blood loss," Erina said, her back to us so she could watch down the hallway in case anyone came.

"There," I said, finished.

Hunter smiled. "Thanks."

One of the enemy men rounded the corner, catching us off guard.

Hunter immediately moved into action. He punched the man in the face, knocking the glasses off, and dealt several body blows to the semi-stunned man as well. The man tried to grapple with Hunter, which was a huge mistake. Hunter quickly tossed the man on the ground, then straddled him, after a few seconds, Hunter had rearranged them so that he had him in a chokehold. The man tried to elbow Hunter, but Hunter was used to that and held on. After a few more attempts to break free, the man passed out. Hunter held on a tad longer, making sure he was actually unconscious before he pushed the man off him and stood.

"That was awesome," Marlee said and fanned her face.

Hunter chuckled.

"Hopefully, you didn't hurt your wound more," I said and tried to check the bandage, but Hunter just patted my shoulder.

"I'm fine. I've taken way worse. He only managed to land

a few punches and luckily didn't know I was injured so he didn't hit me there. There's still one more behind us, so we need to move forward to get to the guys before backup arrives."

I knew Hunter was right, but I couldn't keep myself from worrying. I was more worried about my husbands, though, so I grabbed our stuff and let Hunter take the lead while I took rear.

Walking backwards, handgun at the ready, I couldn't stop wondering what was happening to everyone.

If we'd had more time, I would have tried to get some surveillance inside the meeting rooms, but was fairly certain they wouldn't have cameras in there. Next time, I would force them to wear devices with hidden cameras so we could see what was going on. No, I knew they wouldn't do that, but an overprotective wife could hope.

"Left at the end of this hallway," Erina whispered, providing directions based on the tracking app.

"Who picked this wallpaper?" I asked, looking at the hideous floral wallpaper that reminded me of the 1970s. "Isn't this supposed to be a ritzy hotel?"

"It's just as ugly as the carpet," Marlee commented.

We all looked down and I chuckled. "They need a new interior designer."

"For what we pay them just for Mafia Weekend, they could afford to upgrade," Erina said. "Maybe I'll have a word with the manager when we leave."

"Yes, so sorry about shooting up your hotel, but you really need to change your carpet and wallpaper. I was embarrassed to even shoot people surrounded by this grotesque view," I said.

Marlee and Erina chuckled. Despite everything, it was good to get them to laugh a little as we faced unknown dangers.

"Are all of them still together?" I asked in a whisper.

Erina stopped walking and I would have run into the back of Marlee if she hadn't put her hand on my shoulder to warn me.

"Two of the dots are in a different spot now, but not far. It looks like maybe they moved them to a room next door to the one they were in, I think? Not sure, since this app doesn't know the room layouts, but they're close enough that's what I would think happened."

"Do we go for them first? Or continue to the main group?" Hunter asked.

Having them separated was far from ideal. If we rescued one set before the other, they might kill the others. We didn't have enough people to split our party to rescue them simultaneously, either. On one hand, it would be nice to have more people to fight, but I couldn't be certain that they wouldn't hear the gunfire or fighting and hurt the others. It felt like a lose-lose situation. If we went for the smaller group they could kill the larger group, but if we went for the larger group they could kill the smaller group. Which option was better? How could we rescue everyone without anyone dying?

"Amelia?" Marlee asked softly.

"I'm not sure," I admitted and turned around to look at them all. "What do you guys think?"

"I think we might need to split our party and attack at the same time," Erina said.

"Marlee isn't a fighter, so I'm not sure that's a good idea," I said. Smiling I added, "No offense."

"None taken," she said and gave me a weary smile back.

"If Hunter and Erina go together and Marlee and I go together, that's our best split up. But ... I don't know. If there are way more enemies in one room than the other, it could be catastrophic for that pair."

"You know I don't like the idea of splitting up, but I don't know that we can sneak into any of the rooms to rescue them without alerting the others," Hunter said.

"Who is it that's separated?" I asked Erina.

She scowled. "I'm not sure what these mean. I could probably guess, but..." She handed me the phone back.

I'd assigned them each an ID. Stephan was BB, for billionaire boss. Shea was OX, for his nickname Ox. Arcadio was AA for his A-plus ass, but I'd told him it was for being an A-plus assassin. Forrest was FF, not for Forrest Flowers, but for fantastic fuck, he'd loved that moniker and had bragged about it for weeks. Dane was TD, for twin dimples, but he was one hundred percent certain I had meant for it to be terrific dick. I gave up arguing about it and let him have that one.

OX and AA were the ones separated. If I was Angel Eyes, I would have moved those two to a different room to try to keep the more aggressive, better fighters out of the same room where they were dealing with the bosses. Shea and Arcadio were definitely the more aggressive when it came to defending Stephan's honor. Not that Forrest and Dane wouldn't, they were just more level-headed in dealing with things, usually because they let Stephan set the mood and pace in reactions. Shea and Arcadio acted first then apologized to Stephan after.

"I think we should try to rescue the two separated first," I said, after thinking about why they might have been separated. "It's likely that Alexi and Blain are with them as well."

"Why do you think that?" Hunter asked.

"It's Shea and Arcadio that were separated. If I'm right, they probably moved the more protective, aggressive men into that separate room to give them more time for whatever they're doing with less yelling and threatening from those men," I explained.

"If that is why they moved them, they definitely would have put Alexi and Blain there, too," Erina agreed.

"If we can get them out without alerting the other room, we would have at least two more fighters, possibly four or more, which would definitely help us getting into the other room and taking them down. We have enough weapons to share them as well. Plus, we could go back and collect the guns from the guys we've killed, too, if necessary, before going in."

"You really are pretty smart about these kinds of things," Marlee commented. "I can see why Stephan allows you to go on missions with them now. I wouldn't be able to come up with plans or consider what others might be thinking like you do. Of all the things I've witnessed with you, this has definitely been the most impressive."

For some reason, her praise made me want to cry; tears burned in my eyes, but I refused to let them fall. Maybe it was because of her being older, more experienced in the mafia world. Maybe it was just nice to be praised for something others might be afraid of, but whatever reason, it made me feel warm inside. "Thank you."

"Let's grab the guns off the two at the end of this hallway before we try to rescue Shea and Arcadio," Hunter said.

I nodded. "Good idea."

Once the guns were secured, we headed to the next hallway, which was empty, but as we neared the next intersection, we could hear voices.

Creeping forward, we waited out of sight to hear what they were saying.

"I'm telling you that the wives are here and they killed some of our guys!" one of the men said.

"Listen to yourself," another male voice said and scoffed. "The wives? You think those pampered bitches would break in here and attack us?"

"The other teams haven't caught them yet," a new male voice countered.

"Yeah, because they're probably hiding in a safe room, clinging to each other, crying, and upset that they broke a nail escaping. You all obviously haven't seen these women. They're pretty play things. That's it," the second one said.

"I'm telling you, they shot at us and killed Paolo, Austin, and Bud," the first one snapped.

"Fine, show me the bodies as proof then," the second one challenged.

"We can't leave this door unguarded," the third voice quickly replied, worry in his voice.

"There are two guys inside. Even if those women did

manage to kill a few of our guys, they're not going to be able to break in, kill two more, and escape. They aren't assassins," the second guy replied. "Come on, let's go find the bodies and then maybe I'll agree to go tell the boss."

We plastered ourselves against the wall as their footsteps grew closer.

I held my gun at my chest, ready to shoot if they spotted us.

The three men walked by, completely missing us as they walked down the hallway away from the door that led to Arcadio and Shea.

We waited until they turned the next corner before we hurried to the door to go in.

I waved at Marlee and Erina to stand off to the side of the door, against the walls of the hallway, out of the way.

Hunter took point with me ready right behind him. He counted down from three on his fingers, and when the countdown finished, he threw open the door, stepping inside and to the right.

Two men sat in chairs at the back of the room playing cards, their weapons on the table.

Before they could reach for their weapons, Hunter and I shot them.

I got a headshot while he shot the other person in the chest. Jumping over the table between us and them, Hunter shot the man again, making sure he didn't get back up.

"Clear," I whispered, just loud enough for Marlee and Erina to hear.

They came into the room, shutting and locking the door

behind them so if the others returned, they wouldn't know anything was amiss at first.

On the ground, Shea, Alexi, Arcadio, and Blain, along with four other men I didn't know, were hogtied and gagged.

All of the men looked at us with wide eyes.

I smiled down at Shea. "Hey, handsome. I didn't know you were into bondage. If you'd told me, we could have spiced things up in the bedroom."

Marlee made a gagging sound and Erina groaned.

"Your jokes get cornier and cornier, I swear," Erina said.

Shea rolled his eyes at me.

Removing the dagger from my leg sheath, I cut the ropes securing Shea while Hunter, Erina, and Marlee cut the other men's.

I looked at the four I didn't know and asked, "Should we let them free? They could be decoys."

Marlee bent to free one of them. "This one is from my family."

Once free, Shea untied the gag from his mouth. "They're good. Free them, too." He wrapped his large arms around me and squeezed. "What are you doing here, Kitten?"

"I'm rescuing my husbands," I answered and kissed his neck since it was the only place I could reach. "Someone has to help you, poor, defenseless men. Are you injured?"

He shook his head. "Just hit us to knock us out. No bullet wounds for either of us."

Well, that was a relief.

He released me and Arcadio stepped forward. "You look amazing, my little goddess." His eyes dropped to my hands. "Is that blood on your hands? Are *you* injured?"

"Hunter got grazed by a bullet, so I had to bandage him," I replied as I looked at the smear of blood on my hands. "I did also shoot a few people, so there's also metaphorical blood on my hands if that's what you meant."

He pulled me into a deep kiss, his tongue sweeping across mine and his hand burying in my hair. I slid my hands up his neck, into his thick hair, and gripped it just enough at the scalp to make him press his body closer to mine. Kissing Arcadio was enough to distract me from almost anything. Nothing existed, but he and I in this moment.

"While that was hot to watch, we've got to get moving," Erina said, snapping me out of my haze.

"Right, sorry," I said as I stepped back from Arcadio, but reached down to hold his hand. Shea took my other hand. "Tell us what happened," I ordered no one in particular.

Alexi was the first to speak. "Collman showed up with a group of people, some from each of the families. He walked into the conference room, guns out, and they locked the doors behind them. Before we could do much, they had enough guns pointed at us that we had to stop or risk the bosses getting shot."

"What does Angel Eyes want?" I asked.

Shea sighed. "We don't know. Arcadio and I got a little out of hand when Collman mentioned you, so they moved us to this room."

"Me?" I asked.

Arcadio's hand tightened in mine. "He offered to buy you again, more money this time, and then threatened he was just going to take you, so getting money for you was a better deal for Stephan."

I scoffed. "Clearly, he doesn't know me."

"Clearly," Shea said and squeezed my hand.

I looked up at him and smiled. "Well, they did try to kill me, so I don't think the henchmen are following his orders."

Shea scowled. "What?"

"They tried to kidnap Marlee, not Amelia," Erina explained. "Then tried to kill us after that failed."

"I'm going to murder them all," Blain said in a deadly, quiet voice.

"I think Yaconelli is involved," I said. "He was at the hotel where we were before the meeting."

Shea stepped in front of me. "Yaconelli was at the hotel you were at and you didn't notify us?"

"I tried to tell her we should have notified you, but she didn't want to," Hunter said.

I turned and narrowed my eyes at him. "Throw me under the bus, why don't you?"

"If Yaconelli is in on it, that must be why they didn't put any of his guys in here," Shea said. "I thought it was just because they weren't as aggressive as the rest of us."

"They all just raised their hands in the air, so I thought they were all afraid," Arcadio added.

"What's the plan?" Shea asked and looked at me.

"You're asking her?" one of the random men asked, obviously surprised.

I turned to face him, put one hand on my hip, and cocked it to the side. "Are you forgetting who just rescued your ass?"

"How did you find us anyway?" Blain asked.

"She lo-jacked her husbands," Erina said with a snicker.

"I thought it was hilarious at first, but it sounds like a great idea to me now."

"Do you know where the others are?" Arcadio asked.

I nodded and pointed to the left. "They're in that room still." I held up my phone and showed them the dots together.

Looking around, I was excited to see there was a door that led into the next room. "Here's my plan," I said, a huge smile growing on my face. "We're going to split into two groups. One group will go in the main doors, while another group goes in through this side door. That way no one can escape and we can surprise them from two directions, so they won't be able to just shoot everyone who comes through the main doors. The group going in the side doors should wait until they hear commotion inside, so we have the element of surprise."

"How do you want to split the groups?" Shea asked.

"I want to go through the main doors," I answered. "If he is trying to steal me, he might pause in shooting us if he sees me first, which will give us that moment of hesitation we need."

"You want to step through the door in the front, exposing yourself to possibly getting shot in the face?" Arcadio asked incredulously.

"Yep," I chirped with a huge smile.

"She really is crazy," Blain said.

I winked at him. "All the best women are."

"Only one problem, we don't have weapons," Marlee's guy said.

Hunter picked up the duffel bag he'd dropped at some

point, and set it on the table, opening it so they could see inside. "She thought ahead for that as well."

I set my handgun down and grabbed the shotgun instead. "Mine."

Arcadio and Shea rolled their eyes.

Arcadio reached over and grabbed the handgun that had belonged to one of the guys that had been guarding them.

Shea took the handgun I'd set down and checked it. When he noticed me glaring at him, he just winked at me.

I took my cell phone and sent a message to Mom: Husbands kidnapped. Angel Eyes making his move. Send backup. At the hotel. Activate house lockdown.

I sent her a text with the address next. Hopefully, Randolph could find access to the building and help us or get our high-level mafia members to come and attempt a rescue. Once I was certain it was delivered, I erased the message so if Angel Eyes somehow managed to capture us, he wouldn't know I'd warned my mom.

Done, I handed the phone to Shea, who slipped it into the inner pocket of his suit jacket.

"Marlee, make sure you stay behind him," I said and nodded at her guy. "I don't want you getting shot."

She nodded. "I know. After this, I'm definitely going to spend more time in the shooting range."

I loaded the shotgun with shells and made sure my ninja stars were still in my bra and reachable.

Marlee and Erina each took a shotgun and loaded theirs as well.

"What you got in there?" Arcadio asked, looking down at my cleavage.

"A surprise for later," I said and winked.

His eyes darkened with desire and he took a step towards me, but I stepped over to make sure Marlee's shotgun had the safety off and was ready to go.

"Alright, let's go before reinforcements get here," I said once everyone had loaded weapons at the ready.

Shea opened the door to lead us out, pausing when it was a few inches wide to check if the cost was clear. After a moment, he nodded and stepped out. I followed behind him with Arcadio behind me. We moved down the hallway and around to the entrance to the other room. The fact the entrance wasn't right next to this one was frustrating, but there was nothing we could do about that. Once there, we found two guards outside of it. Shea quickly dispatched them and we stepped up to the doors.

"You sure about this?" he asked, his jaw tight.

I jumped up and kissed his cheek. "Yes."

Arcadio kissed my cheek and said, "We're going to start shooting the ones we know are enemies as soon as we walk in. Don't hesitate."

I nodded and raised my shotgun up, one hand on the pump and one wrapped around with a finger on the trigger.

Shea and Arcadio each grabbed a door handle, counted down silently, and jerked them all the way open.

Chapter 12

Amelia

I stepped through the doors and immediately shot the man in front of us, the one who'd escaped earlier and had tried to warn them that we were here.

The room was spacious and well-lit, with large windows offering stunning views of the city skyline. On the walls, there are several large framed paintings, adding a touch of sophistication to the space. The room is also equipped with state-of-the-art technology, including a large screen at the front of the room for presentations and video conferences. The room was air-conditioned and the temperature was just right, creating a comfortable atmosphere for meetings that could sometimes last for hours. The centerpiece of the room was a large, oval conference table, made of polished mahogany wood and surrounded by plush leather chairs.

The executive conference room was an impressive space that was well-suited for any high-level meeting or presentation. The attention to detail and luxurious amenities made it clear that this hotel truly valued its guests and their comfort. Unlike the hallway to get here with its awful carpet and wallpaper, this room had dark brown carpet and dark, cherry wood walls.

All of the bosses were tied to highbacked executive chairs, seated around the conference table. Angel Eyes and men I didn't recognize were all standing, holding weapons, which made it easier to see who the enemies were. The guards were tied to chairs pushed up against the walls.

Shea and Arcadio started shooting. Blain and Alexi came out blasting from the side room as well.

Within a few minutes, most of the enemies were dead, and the rest had dropped their weapons and cowered on the floor with their hands raised.

Angel Eyes stared at me with a look that seemed to be both shocked and aroused at the same time. Yeah, I tended to have that effect on men. "Mrs. Moriarty, we weren't expecting you."

Angel Eyes stood near the head of the conference table, just to the left of Stephan. I didn't like him being so close to my husband when he was tied up. I needed to get him away from him quickly. Shooting him from here with the shotgun wasn't a good idea, the shot could spread and hit Stephan and Brian, too. I needed to get closer.

Forrest and Dane were situated opposite Stephan, their heads bloody from what looked like being hit with the butt of a gun. Stephan didn't appear to have any wounds, thankfully. Connor and Brian didn't appear to be wounded either.

"I heard you were trying to buy me again, so why wouldn't I come to discuss the matter?" I said, and leaned the shotgun up against my shoulder. Striding forward with long steps that had my high slit going up even higher, I approached.

Angel Eyes took in my dress, his eyes roving from my toes to the top of my head. *That's right, focus on me.*

I looked at Stephan, who was smiling proudly. "How much did he offer you this time, dear husband?"

"Not enough, I'm afraid," Stephan replied.

I tsked. "I don't know that that's for you to decide."

Stephan's smile grew. "Of course, how misogynistic of me. I would have called you, but as you can see, I've been a little tied up."

A snort of laughter came out of me and I slapped my free hand over my mouth to stop it.

Erina groaned. "You've infected Stephan with your corniness, too?"

Angel Eyes started to turn towards Erina, but I quickly spoke again.

"So, aside from trying to purchase me, what else has been going on in here?" I looked at the others. "None of these bosses have any say over me." My eyes found Yaconelli's, and I saw that he, too, was tied up. "Yaconelli, it was nice bumping into you earlier tonight. So unexpected of you and Collman to be at the Gregori's casino the same night you had this meeting."

Glancing at Stephan, I saw the smile fade into a scowl as he grasped the meaning of my comment.

Angel Eyes clapped his hands. "Very perceptive. I hadn't thought you'd spotted me in the crowded casino. I wasn't supposed to get close to you at all while there, but your beauty always draws me in. To answer your question, Amelia …"

I did not like to hear him use my first name.

"… I was simply trying to discuss business with them as a fellow mafia boss, and they reacted violently. So, I had to protect myself. You understand?"

I walked closer to him, smiled, and nodded. "I do understand what you're saying, but you have to understand where they're coming from also."

He arched a brow. "Pardon?"

"Well, you've been stealing members from all of our families, attempting to sabotage our businesses, and tried to assassinate the bosses' wives. Who wouldn't want to kill you after all of that? Plus, you offered my husband money to buy me, but your henchmen tried to kill me on the way here. That seems a little counterintuitive, don't you think?"

He frowned. "I ordered them to kidnap you, not kill you." He sighed, took a few steps away from Stephan and said, "It's so hard to find good help these days. I'm sorry they tried to harm you."

I dipped my head in acknowledgement. "Apology accepted." Well, at least we knew now that they hadn't been after Marlee, which was likely a relief to her.

"I have a question though, if you knew I was responsible for all of that, why not try to come after me?" He put his hands in his pockets, completely at ease, despite having several guns trained on him. How could he be so calm? Did he have some backup plan, or did he think we just wouldn't kill him?

I shrugged one shoulder and reached up into my bra,

opening the case to access the ninja stars. It likely looked as though I were itching my boob. "It's about the long game, Mr. Collman."

"Is that why you've kept me talking instead of killing me? Stalling for time for backup to arrive?"

I was close enough now that I could shoot him. I scoffed, pulled out a ninja star, and said, "I've got all the backup I need right here." Throwing the ninja star at his face made him duck down, which gave me the perfect opportunity to raise my shotgun and shoot him right between the eyes.

I shot him one more time, just to be sure... always double tap... and turned around to face the room with a smile. "Now, why don't we get back to business?"

"Ah, but the business hasn't even started yet," Angel Eyes said from behind us.

I spun around, eyes wide, fear pounding through me as I looked at the dead Angel Eyes on the floor and the very much alive one standing in the doorway.

At some point, he and more men had done the exact same thing we'd done to them, coming in through both entry points and cornering us.

"Wh-What?" I gaped.

The alive Angel Eyes strode in, taking off a pair of leather gloves. "I'm a bit disappointed, Mrs. Moriarty. I'd at least hoped you would notice he was a body double, not truly myself. I'd thought we had a better connection." He tsked. "Perhaps the feelings are too one-sided for us to last, even if Stephan would agree to sell you."

What could we do? If we started shooting, we might

defeat all these men, but some of ours would get shot, too. I couldn't let Arcadio or Shea die.

"What do you want?" I asked. "And don't say me, because we both know you didn't go through all of this just for me. You could have kidnapped me or hired people to kidnap me instead of this."

He smiled. "You continue to make yourself more attractive to me. Yes, I do have another agenda, but first, why don't we get more comfortable. It can't have been easy getting across town and killing a dozen of my men, in heels and a dress. Please, take a seat."

He grabbed an empty chair from the wall next to him and pushed it so that it rolled across the carpet towards me.

Arcadio and Shea still had their weapons in their hands, we all did, but I gave them one discreet shake of my head as I grabbed the chair and pulled it to sit right beside Stephan. I set the shotgun on top of my lap and smiled. "Thank you, my feet were getting sore from standing so much."

"Please, the rest of you should take seats as well," he said, smiling like a magnanimous ruler.

The men who'd surrendered earlier grabbed their weapons and stood back up, adding more guns against us.

"You look stunning," Stephan said and leaned over to kiss my cheek. "Your display was wonderful as well. Very arousing."

I smiled and reached over to set a hand on his upper thigh, partly as a show of affection and mainly to try to untie his hands, if possible. "Thank you."

Arcadio bent down and kissed my cheek, one hand dropping to my lap where he slid a two-inch dagger under my dress's slit. "That ninja star throw was very hot," he said as an excuse before he took a seat beside Dane.

Instead of immediately using the dagger, I waited, needing to make sure Angel Eyes didn't suspect anything.

I looked at him and smiled. "Could I get some water, too? I'm a little parched."

Angel Eyes smiled and nodded. "Of course, how could I forget something so simple. Get everyone some water, please." He said it while staring at me, but one of the men behind him immediately went over to a cabinet on the far wall and opened one door, revealing a small refrigerator with bottles of water.

Angel Eyes waited until we all had our water, but none of the bosses could drink it. I unscrewed the lid from one and held it up so Stephan could drink. Erina and Marlee did the same for their husbands.

After I took my drink and set the bottle down, Angel Eyes asked, "Are you ready now?"

I nodded. "Yes, thank you for your hospitality."

Out of the corner of my eye I saw Dane roll his eyes.

When dealing with megalomaniacs, praise was the best option.

Angel Eyes smiled. "Wonderful. Now, let's talk about territory." He snapped his fingers.

One man carried in a laptop, which another man helped set up, and connect to the presentation screen. Once connected, they immediately put a map of the country on the screen. It had territories outlined for all of the bosses in the room.

"As you can see," Angel Eyes said, "you all currently own

most of the good territories. I think it's safe to say none of us care about the boonies. However, that makes it quite difficult for a new family to move in." He hit a button and the map changed, this time showing a huge square right in the center of ours, Yaconelli's, Gregori's, and Torreto's territories. A much larger portion came from Torreto's than ours, and a smaller portion from Yaconelli's.

"You want us to give up the downtown areas, arguably the best areas, to you?" Connor asked.

"Well, I can't exactly have an operation running around you, can I? Well, I could, but that's way too cumbersome," Angel Eyes replied.

"You're taking twice as much from me as Yaconelli," Brian said.

"Ah, yes, well that's because Yaconelli offered that bit to me without question. You are weakening and can't really defend all of that territory anymore. So, it makes sense for you to give me more."

"No," Brian said immediately.

Angel Eyes sighed. "This is a negotiation, not a dictatorship. Try to be reasonable, Mr. Torreto."

"As you said, you're new," I interrupted. "Do you really think just because you stole a few of our men, not even our good ones, that you'll be able to protect all those territories? As a new boss to this area, it's more practical for you to take over a smaller area for now. Expansion can be discussed again at the next Mafia Weekend."

He smiled. "You forget I'm not new, though."

"No, but you're new to this area. Just because things have

been going well for a few months doesn't mean you can sustain this for years."

His smile grew. "You are quite intoxicating when you speak so knowledgably about the business. How can I bribe you to come to my side? Riches? Cars? I'll pay you the one billion I offered your husband to become my wife and help me run this family."

"One billion?" I scoffed. "You think so little of me. And clearly, you've forgotten that I am a main component of our legitimate business, doing interviews and adding my face next to Stephan's for the public eye as well. I've brought over half a billion dollars in sales just from one of my inventions to our company."

I wasn't saying it to brag, but so often men like him forgot that a mafia wife could provide so much more than just beauty and sex. I wasn't a toy. I was a legitimate partner to my husband.

"You drive a hard bargain," he said and frowned.

"I know my worth," I said. "It took me a long time to accept and realize my worth and it's something not a lot of women ever do. So, let's be more practical," I said. "You let us leave right now, and we'll give you two blocks of main street, plus five blocks of the east side. Prove you can hold and run that area and we'll be open to negotiating more. That along with the territory Yaconelli gave you is plenty for a new boss."

Angel Eyes frowned, his mouth pulling down deep at the corners. "Now you're the one thinking too little of the other person. That's an insulting offer. Plus, your husband hasn't consented to it."

"My wife is perfectly capable of negotiating on my

behalf," Stephan said. "Although I'd rather shoot you in the face than give you territory, I understand my hands are tied." He held his hands up as if to prove that point.

I grabbed the dagger from between my legs and moved it back into his lap, his movement the perfect opportunity to act as though I was simply moving my hand out of the way so he could raise his. Sometimes, my husband was incredibly brilliant.

"What about you, Mr. Gregori?" Angel Eyes asked.

Connor considered him a moment, quiet and intense as he looked at the map and Angel Eyes. "I will give you two blocks of downtown that connects to Moriarty's."

Angel Eyes continued to frown. "Two? That's it?"

"Take it or leave it," Connor said and smiled. "It's more than I would have given were circumstances different, however, like Stephan, I can understand when negotiations are necessary."

I started using the dagger to cut the ropes on Stephan's hands, making my movements as discreet as possible.

"Mr. Torreto, have you reconsidered your situation now that you've heard from your friends?" Angel Eyes asked.

Brian clenched his jaw and stared at the table a long, quiet moment. "I'm not giving you any of my territory." He looked up, glaring. "That's not negotiable."

Angel Eyes sighed and stood. "I was worried Mr. Gregori would be the problem, but clearly it's you." He grabbed a gun from one of his men and aimed it at Brian.

I didn't think. I just reacted.

I threw the dagger and it sunk into Angel Eyes' hand, making him drop the handgun.

"Sir! We are supposed to be civilized! Killing him because you didn't get the answer you want is childish," I snapped to cover up my action. My heart pounded in my chest, a mixture of fear and excitement.

Several of his men aimed their guns at me.

Stephan and the rest of my husbands tensed, not liking so many weapons aimed at me.

He clutched his bleeding hand to his chest and glared at me. "You little—"

"I could have thrown it at your head or face, but I hit your hand. I also could have shot you with my shotgun, but I didn't. Accept the mercy I just bestowed upon you," I said, heart hammering even harder at the lie. I literally hadn't considered throwing it anywhere else; I just wanted to keep Brian alive.

"Let me bandage that," one of the men said, stepping forward with a first aid kit.

I took my seat again, adjusting the shotgun on my lap.

Marlee looked at me with tear-filled eyes, thanking me silently.

Brian dipped his head once to me.

I gave him a glare, trying to convey that he needed to play along as well.

He narrowed his eyes and leaned back in his seat.

Stubborn ass men!

Why couldn't he see that he needed to play along to keep him and Marlee alive? We could destroy Angel Eyes later.

Retreating to fight another day was perfectly acceptable.

"Do you have a printed version of the map?" I asked. "So

we can draw on it to indicate the areas we're giving you so you can see your new territory?"

Angel Eyes was still glaring at me, but he jerked his head at a nearby man. "Get a printed version and markers as she requested."

I smiled and said, "See, isn't it so much better when we're all being civilized?"

Thankfully, the dagger hadn't gone through his hand, and had actually fallen out when he'd flinched, so they could bandage it without needing to immediately go to the hospital.

"Can I have my dagger back?" I asked politely.

"No, I think I'll keep this as a souvenir," Angel Eyes said. "You're the first women to ever throw a knife at me."

I pouted, sticking my bottom lip out as far as I could. "But that's my favorite dagger. It reminds me why I'm lucky to have the men I do."

He looked down at the dagger, frowning, then narrowed his eyes, understanding I was making a big dick joke.

Forrest coughed to cover up his laugh, as did Alexi.

Erina turned her head so Angel Eyes couldn't see her and smiled at me.

Chapter 13

Amelia

"Bring in some food," Angel Eyes ordered the man next to him. "I'm hungry."

"So, I have to ask, why did you come all the way to this side of the country? Why not just expand on the Eastern side?" I asked him, wanting to keep him talking.

My phone chimed in Shea's pocket, drawing everyone's attention.

"Give it," Angel Eyes ordered, ignoring my question now that my phone had distracted him.

Shea handed it to the man who came over.

"That's mine," I announced. "I had Shea hold it since this dress doesn't exactly have pockets."

Angel Eyes opened it and frowned. "Your mother is telling you about a sale?"

My mouth popped open and eyes widened. "Oh, can you read it? If it's for my favorite makeup, I need to make sure I get onto their website as soon as the sale starts. I'm a sucker for a good sale."

"Sales, really? You're a billionaire," he countered.

"I grew up poor, sir. Pinching pennies is still deeply ingrained in me. Can you please read it? Please. Please."

He frowned, staring at me to see if this was a ploy somehow, which it totally was, and finally read it. "Thirty percent off sale for Mr. E's with limited online options starting three slash twenty-eight. In-person purchases have more options."

Thirty minutes until they would arrive. Three teams with a total of twenty-eight people. They didn't have enough visual surveillance, so they were coming in mostly blind. Thank you, Mom.

I squealed. "Oh, how exciting! Mr. E has the most gorgeous eyeshadows!"

"Is that the one you brought tonight?" Erina asked, playing along.

I nodded. "Yes, that palette!"

"Oh, I need to buy during that sale, too. Hun, can I use my card to buy some?" she asked Connor.

"Don't you have enough eyeshadow?" he asked, acting very put out.

"Excuse me?" she demanded.

"What he meant to say is that of course we'll let you use the card to buy more eyeshadow. You're just so beautiful without makeup that it confuses us why you want more makeup, but if it makes you happy, then it makes us happy," Damien said. It was the first time he'd talked so far, and I was actually shocked he replied.

"I love the one palette I have from him," Marlee said. "I definitely need to buy some more during the sale."

Brian sighed. "Really? More?"

"Did you hear Damien? You should respond more like him," she said and glared at Brian.

Brian sighed again. "Right. I'm sorry. Please, buy all you want, love."

She smiled and straightened. "Thank you."

"We should make a day of it," I said. "Mimosas and sales!"

"Yes!" Erina and Marlee shouted simultaneously.

I was so happy these girls played along with me so well. They had no idea what the text meant, but my husbands and I did.

"Are they always like this?" Angel Eyes asked.

"Yes," Brian, Connor, and Stephan replied immediately with exasperation clear in their tones.

One of the men returned carrying a tray of food containing sandwiches, chips, and cookies.

The sandwiches were the premade kind in plastic containers, so they were probably safe to eat, but I wasn't certain I wanted to take that risk. Plus, it was really late, so I wasn't too hungry.

Angel Eyes was the only one who took food from the tray, but he didn't seem to mind that the rest of us weren't eating.

After a few tense minutes of silence, the man returned with the printed map, but it was only a regular sheet of paper in size.

"You couldn't have printed it larger?" I asked, annoyed. With a sigh, I waved my hand at the laptop. "Give me that. I can just make the notes on there instead."

Angel Eyes' lips twitched, but he didn't allow the smile to form. "Give her the laptop," he ordered the man.

Once on the table in front of me, I opened the image of the map of our territories as they currently were in a photo editing software. Using a pen tool, I took a different color from the rest of ours to make it easily discernable, and traced out the areas we'd indicated so far we were willing to give up to Angel Eyes.

"Mr. Yaconelli, can you please tell me what areas you agreed to give Mr. Collman?"

He told me the areas and I colored them in.

Looking at the map now, I pointed to a section of Brian's territory that was near the area Yaconelli had given to Angel Eyes. I was fairly certain it wasn't a truly necessary area for Brian and Marlee's business, losing a few blocks wouldn't seriously affect them. If Brian gave him a few blocks there, that would also connect Angel Eyes' territory, so there would be no splits.

"What about this area?" I asked Brian.

His jaw clenched and he was quiet so long I thought he was ignoring me. Marlee set her hand on his forearm. After another few seconds, he sighed. "Fine. Petunia Street to Daffodil Lane and Market Street to Charger Road."

It took me a minute to find the ones he'd indicated, but once I did, I highlighted them and sat back with a smile. "See, this is a decent-sized territory by anyone's standards."

He scowled at the projector screen, staring at the high-lighted area.

Honestly, it was a very small area, but he was coming in and taking it by force, so he shouldn't expect more. If he demanded more, I wasn't really certain what I could do. At this moment, he had us by the horns, but the moment we got home, we would do everything in our power to destroy him. And I was certain he knew that.

If he could kill us all right here and now, that would destabilize our families, businesses, and give him the opportunity he needed to swoop in and take over. He might be smart, but I couldn't see him being able to handle all of our territories. I think that's why he was targeting Brian earlier, but that was an assumption. He knew killing Stephan would cause international scandal and would make it harder to accomplish his goals. Killing Connor would cause issues because his family was fiercely loyal to him, much more than any of the others. Everyone from his officers down to the pawns would rally to take revenge. Brian, however, didn't have as loyal of a group, he wasn't as well known publicly as Connor or Stephan, and Brian did have a smaller territory. One that Angel Eyes was already destabilizing.

"While I appreciate the visual and offers, they aren't enough," Angel Eyes finally said and looked at Stephan. "I want half of the west side."

I wanted to tell him he was crazy and go take a long walk off a short pier, but I wasn't certain what his reaction would be. I couldn't risk him killing Stephan or the others. How could I protect my family?

"That's far too large of my territory to give you, plus, I have essential businesses located there," Stephan said. "Public companies that are very well known."

"You all seem to forget that I am in charge at this moment. Your next breath is not guaranteed," Angel Eyes snapped and stood.

I stood as well, aiming the shotgun at him. "Don't."

His men aimed their weapons at me, which made Arcadio and Shea stand and aim their weapons at some of them.

Alexi, Blain, Marlee's guy, and one of the others also drew their weapons.

The tense standoff was not good. If one of these guys was trigger happy, it could spell disaster.

Just as I opened my mouth, the doors opened, which had several of Angel Eyes' men turning to aim at the newcomers.

My eyes widened as I watched my father, Stanley, walk in wearing a suit. He didn't even pause when he saw our standoff, or when some of those weapons turned in his direction.

"Can I help you?" Angel Eyes asked. "I think you have the wrong room."

"You must be Mr. Collman," Stanley said.

"And you are?" he asked back.

"Stanley Marvél," my father answered with a smile, walking by him without even extending his hand, and heading towards me.

Chapter 14

Marlee

Several eyes widened at the announcement, since he was supposed to be dead or missing.

Stanley walked over to Amelia and kissed her cheek. "Good evening, Amelia."

"It's a pleasant surprise to see you here, Stanley," she replied with a wide smile, not lowering her weapon from still being aimed at Angel Eyes.

She had been so fast to aim the shotgun, while I had simply frozen.

"I'd shake your hand, but—" Stephan indicated his hands.

Stanley patted Stephan on the shoulder as he walked behind him. "No worries. I see you're a bit tied up."

Shea stood and offered his chair to Stanley.

Stanley patted him on the shoulder. "Thank you, son."

Shea nodded once and went back to his spot on the wall, remaining standing.

Stanley pulled the chair over until he was sitting beside Amelia, one ankle crossed over the opposite knee. His suit was gorgeous, a dark brown, almost black, with silver stripes that caught the light as he moved. I'd met him a few times now, but it was interesting to see how charismatic he was. Even though he hadn't been around Amelia when she was raised, I could see bits of him in her. Perhaps it was genetics, or maybe her mother had inadvertently recreated those traits in her. Sitting side by side, I could also see facial similarities between them I had failed to notice before.

"Mr. Marvél, what are you doing here?" Angel Eyes asked.

Stanley arched a brow. "I'm sorry, are you new? This is Mafia Weekend, I'm a mafia boss, so I'm here to talk business."

A laugh almost slipped out, but I held it in.

"Where do you have territory?" Angel Eyes asked, clearly annoyed at this distraction and possible wrench in his plans. I hoped Stanley had a plan and wasn't winging it as much as we were.

Stanley tapped Amelia's side. "Can you pull up a map of the East Coast?"

She tensed, but didn't move right away, likely not wanting to lower her weapon, if I knew her, and I knew her pretty well. Honestly, the way she'd taken charge once we got in here was freaking impressive. I wouldn't have been able to come up with a plan as quickly as she had.

I still had so much to learn. If whatever Amelia was doing here didn't work, I wasn't sure what we could do. With Brian tied to a chair, there wasn't much I could do to keep him safe. The shotgun on my lap felt like a weight, one that I wasn't sure what to do with. I mean, obviously I knew I could shoot someone with it, but there were so many enemies in this room. It would only take one bullet to lose Brian. I couldn't lose him.

Reluctantly, Amelia lowered her gun, set it on the table, and googled a map of the East Coast.

Stanley reached over and pointed at the screen. "Here through here."

She highlighted the areas and made sure it showed on the screen.

Angel Eyes went from curious to furious. "You are claiming those areas?"

"Yes," Stanley said confidently.

"That's at least half of my territory," Angel Eyes commented.

"Oh, it was, but not in the past four months," Stanley said. "You left, leaving it open for the taking."

There was a tense silence as Angel Eyes absorbed the new information.

Amelia's eyes sparkled and she bit her lower lip, likely trying to keep a comment in that would infuriate Angel Eyes more.

Angel Eyes asked, very softly, "When?"

"As I said, 'four months,'" Stanley replied with a wide smile.

Chapter 15

Amelia

Was I feeling... respect for my father? When did he have the time or knowledge to go after Angel Eyes' area? Had he planned this knowing that he was messing with our areas? I hadn't even spoken to him about this. Did Mom tell him?

"What is it you wish to discuss, Mr. Marvél?" Angel Eyes asked.

"You're trying to encroach on the West Coast, but you can't even handle the East Coast," Stanley said. "I think you should refocus on the areas you can actually handle."

"I've got the bosses of all of the West Coast tied up. I could kill them all," Angel Eyes said calmly.

Stanley narrowed his eyes. "Do you intend to kill the wives as well?"

"Potentially," he admitted with a nonchalant shrug.

Stephan tensed, but said nothing.

Stanley, to his credit, didn't react. "You think you'll be able to deal with the aftermath?" he asked.

"The aftermath will be negligible," Angel Eyes said with a shrug.

He was clearly insane. How could he not think that our families wouldn't react to him killing not just their bosses, but the bosses and their wives-slash-ladies, too?

Stanley sighed and shook his head. "You're young and inexperienced, but I didn't think you were an idiot."

Angel Eyes narrowed his eyes.

Stanley straightened in his seat and clasped his hands in his lap. "Here's my offer: leave the west coast and I'll return the territory I stole."

"And if I refuse?" Angel Eyes asked.

Stanley smiled. "Thirty men will march through those doors and kill all of your men. You will be tied up and taken to a secluded location, where Ox will beat you within an inch of your life; you threatened his wife just now, remember."

Ox straightened where he stood against the wall and I realized he was giving off murder vibes. So hot!

"Finally, we will put your body in the foundation of the new building Stephan is building," Stanley said.

"Why do you care about these people and this side of the country?" Angel Eyes asked.

Stanley tilted his head towards me. "That's my daughter."

"Your daughter?" Angel Eyes asked, eyes wide.

Several others murmured in surprise.

"My only child. So, I'm sure you can understand my irritation when I learned a low-level scrub like you had the audacity to try to purchase her, like she was cattle, and then began threatening her friends and upsetting her. I may have retired, but it doesn't take long to reconnect with old friends, call in some favors, and take over the territory that I did."

My father might have been absent from my life, but he clearly cared for me. I hadn't even told him about those things because I wanted help, and he knew I wasn't asking for help. But he still went out and started taking action. I could see why Mom loved him.

"You're so sweet," I said and sniffled. "You did all that even though I didn't ask for help."

"I took revenge on every single person who wronged your mother. I made sure anyone who looked down their nose at her lost it. You are my one and only child, I could not let this stand, and while I tried to let you handle it yourself, I also wanted to ensure he paid for viewing you as less when you are very clearly superior."

I gave him a firm hug and turned back to look at Angel Eyes.

"What is your answer, Mr. Collman?" Stanley asked.

Angel Eyes stared at us silently. I could hear the wheels turning in his head as he tried to find some way out of this. Some way to stay here and keep his territory on the other side of the country.

It would be nice to have operations on both coasts. It would open a lot more doors for him. He had no way of knowing if Stanley was bluffing about the people outside waiting to come and kill them.

Angel Eyes could try to run, but he also knew if we managed to survive that his days would be numbered. All of his hard work, all of his scheming, all of his money and time had been completely wasted. He was likely out billions of dollars at this point. It was going to be a huge blow to take, one he might not bounce back from. And, knowing that it took my father only four months to infiltrate, and that Stanley had a hold there now also showed him that he wasn't as safe on the East Coast as he thought.

I saw the moment his decision was made and moved as he opened his mouth.

"Kill them all," he said and turned to head for the door.

I stepped out away from the table, aimed, and shot, hitting him in the back. I pumped the shotgun, chambering another round, and shot again. One of his men stepped in the way, gun aimed at me, but the shot hit him before he could shoot me.

Chaos erupted as Shea, Arcadio, and the others on our side still with weapons started shooting at the same time as Angel Eyes' men.

I didn't have time to check on everyone. I had to get him before he could escape. Letting him go meant fear, and I was not going to live my life in fear or allow my friends to be controlled by him any longer. This ended tonight.

Angel Eyes was at the door already, but when he tried to open them, they stayed closed. He pulled harder, but they were clearly locked.

"What's the password?" I heard Augustine, one of our officers, ask from the other side.

"It's over," I told Angel Eyes. "You lost."

He turned around, fury filling his eyes, his breathing erratic.

I pressed the gun into his chest. "Thanks for letting me

kill you twice. This has been a very healing night." I squeezed the trigger before he could respond or react.

Once I was certain he was dead, I spun around to check for casualties on our side.

Hunter was in front of me and immediately exhaled harshly. "He could have grabbed the gun from you or knocked it away. You always have to say something first. Just kill him then say it."

I patted his shoulder. "I'm fine. Thank you." All of my husbands were approaching and none seemed to be bleeding. I skipped over and twirled in front of them. "Was I impressive? Did you enjoy being saved by your wife instead of having to rescue me?"

Shea grabbed me around the waist, lifted me up and kissed me deeply. Once he'd finished, he set me on my feet, turned me around, and swatted my butt. "Next time, don't run across a room where everyone is shooting at each other. You could have gotten shot by someone on accident."

"You were magnificent," Stephan praised me and kissed my cheek.

Forrest, Dane, and Arcadio took turns scolding and kissing me as well.

I pouted. "Next time I'm not going to save you guys if you're just going to nag me."

Marlee pushed between Forrest and Dane and threw her arms around me. "Thank you. Thank you. I fucking owe you big time."

I hugged her back. "You don't owe me anything. Friends are supposed to keep each other alive."

"I always said his stubbornness would be the end of him

and it almost was," she said and sniffled. Stepping back, she turned and pointed her finger at Brian, who was getting the ropes removed from his hands and legs. "You need to learn how to negotiate better."

Stanley walked to the door and tapped on it three times. "Augustine, can you let the team in? There are several bodies that need disposed of." He looked down at Angel Eyes' body blocking the door and opened his mouth to say something about it, but Shea bent, grabbed one of his feet, and dragged him out of the way.

"Did you really take over part of his territory or was it all a bluff?" I asked Stanley.

"Oh, it was one hundred percent true. However, I won't be keeping it. Dealing with this reminded me why I left in the first place. I get enough excitement and drama watching from the sidelines now." He pulled out his phone and called someone. "Yes, we're all done and safe. You can lift the lockdown."

"Thanks, Mom!" I yelled so she could hear.

"She said, 'you're welcome,'" Stanley repeated and walked away to continue talking to her as the rest of our team came inside.

Stephan went over to talk to Yaconelli, who was looking quite nervous now.

Shea followed behind him and Arcadio trailed him.

Forrest walked over to talk to Blain, bumping fists as they spoke.

Dane came up behind me and wrapped his arms around me, resting his chin on top of my head. "Don't ever do that again," he grumbled. "I was so scared they were going to shoot you."

I squeezed his forearm. "I was more worried about them shooting you all, since you were tied up and couldn't even duck under the table or anything."

"It was really hot watching you take charge of the negotiations. You've come a long way since I asked you out at your coffee shop."

I chuckled. "It feels like that was an eternity ago."

He nodded, his chin rubbing against the top of my head. I stepped away and smoothed my hair down, spinning to glare at him. "You're ruining my hair."

He smirked and helped smooth it down. "Sorry."

Erina walked over and hugged me.

"Thank you for playing along with my makeup sale story," I said as I hugged her back.

"What was that about?" she asked and Marlee turned to listen as well.

"It was a coded message from Mom to let me know they were sending people," I explained.

"Ah, that makes sense now why you begged him to read it," Erina said while nodding.

"Any casualties?" I asked her softly.

"One of Yaconelli's men died, but no one on our side," she replied.

I exhaled in relief. "Good."

"So, did you guys even get to discuss anything that was on your agenda?" Erina asked Dane.

Dane shook his head. "Nope, he interrupted us right away. We didn't even get through introductions."

"Wow," I said and chuckled mirthlessly. "He definitely knew his timing. If it weren't for the fact that we needed to call you about the guard trying to kidnap Marlee, we wouldn't have known for who knows how long that you were in trouble."

"It is scary to think about," Erina said softly. "We need an SOS notification somehow that they can activate without phones."

"Our tracking devices might be able to be modified so they can still look like jewelry, but also have emergency buttons, somehow," I said as I looked down at my necklace. "Maybe if it's squeezed longer than three seconds it sends a message to whoever it's programmed to send to." I was ninety percent certain that we could figure it out, and that Stephan would be willing to use some resources to accomplish it. "I'll let you know once we've figured it out."

"Look at you, my little problem-solving inventor," Dane praised and wrapped his arm around my waist, squeezing me against his side.

"I get ten percent of the idea!" Erina said with a serious face. She held it for all of two seconds before laughing.

"Hey, I bought you that purse you'd been eyeing for your help with the app I created," I reminded her. "I'll definitely pay you back for this."

She clasped her hands together and her mouth popped open. "I want the matching wallet!"

I bowed and said, "Your wish is my command."

"You see this!" she yelled and pointed at me, turning to look at her husbands. "This is how you should respond to me! See, Amelia knows how to treat a woman!"

Chapter 16

Marlee

After everything that happened, Connor put everyone up in a room at the casino, then the men met the following day to actually discuss the matters they needed to.

Erina, Amelia, and I spent the day getting massages, manicures, pedicures, and facials. All of our husbands even gave us permission to go on a shopping spree, saying we earned it for our rescue job.

Honestly, I didn't feel like I earned any of it. However, I wasn't going to be the Debbie Downer, and Amelia's infectious excitement spread to me as we began perusing the stores.

"Thank you, again, for everything," I said to Hunter as we waited for Amelia to try on another dress. I was certain it was the hundredth of the day.

He shook his head. "You really don't need to thank me. She did everything. I was just an extra pair of hands."

"You killed the first guy who tried to kidnap me and tackled and killed the second one. Without you, our plan would have failed. Don't be so hesitant to accept your part in things."

He looked at me and arched a brow. "Shouldn't I be saying that to you? You may be decent at hiding it from the others, but I know what a fighter looks like when they think they didn't win legitimately. You did far better than you think yesterday. Just having you with a weapon at our backs helped Amelia and I move forward. Don't sell yourself short."

I smiled at him and felt some of the tension and sadness ease away. "You really are a good listener and friend. I can see why Amelia is fond of you."

His cheeks reddened slightly and he turned away.

Amelia walked out and did a spin in a gorgeous, bright red halter top dress, with a billowy skirt. "What do you think?"

"That's stunning," I said.

Erina stepped out wearing a super deep v-neck dress with a low back that just barely covered her butt. "Oh, that *is* stunning," she agreed.

"You look sexy as fuck!" I shouted a little too loud.

A huge grin spread across Erina's face and she did a twirl. "You think my husbands will like it?"

"I think anyone with eyes will like it," I said. "Seriously, that is *hot*."

"No fair, your dress is sexier than mine," Amelia said and pouted, but then quickly smiled. "You look phenomenal. You sure you had a baby recently?"

Erina twirled again in front of the mirror and smiled. "Yeah, I'm definitely buying this one."

"You should buy that one, too," Hunter told Amelia. "It

will be a great dress to wear to the next function Stephan forces you to go to."

Amelia frowned. "Oh, yeah. We have a fundraiser event next week that he said I have to attend."

"I saw a handbag that will go perfect with that," I said and spun around, hurrying over to the display to grab it.

There were a couple of handbags that would actually pair well with it, but knowing Amelia, she wouldn't keep it on her, or if she did keep it on her, it would need to have a weapon in it. Since I couldn't decide, I grabbed the two I was waffling between, one in each hand, and walked back over to her.

"This one matches the dress and is small, so you could just keep it empty, wear it for style, and leave it on the table with no worry about whether anyone will steal it." I held up the larger, black one. "This one goes well with it, and is large enough for one of your small daggers or that tiny gun you usually wear on your ankle."

She looked back and forth between them and tapped her lips. "You're right, the bigger one is big enough for a weapon and still looks stylish enough to go with the dress. They won't even bother to open it when we go inside. So, I could have my thigh dagger, boob shuriken, and my small pistol in the bag." Holding the bag she'd chosen against her side, she turned each way to examine her reflection. Satisfied, she turned back around and smiled wide. "You know me so well. Thanks, Mar!"

Warmth bloomed in my chest at her thanks and at the realization that I *did* know her so well.

I threw my arms around her and squeezed tight. "I love you."

She returned my hug. "I love you, too."

"Hey!" Erina complained and hurried over to hug us both. "I love you two, too."

Laughing, we stood in each other's embrace for longer than we normally would. Living through the chaos of yesterday, surviving thanks to each other, had made our bond even stronger.

"You think next time you get pregnant Connor will let us come over now?" I asked.

Erina snorted and Amelia laughed.

"I think he won't have a foot to stand on if he tries that shit again after all of this," Erina said.

We stepped back and they went to change.

Finally, I felt like things were going right, and I felt more complete than I ever had before. I'd thought that Brian was all I needed, but these women proved to me that I needed more. I had been lacking a family and they were now providing me that.

I'd gone from life with just Brian and our mafia family, to becoming an aunt to three adorable children from two different sisters, and I'd gained nine brothers, ten if I counted Hunter, which after all of this, I definitely did.

My personal life was great, and with Collman out of the way, I could finally relax a bit.

"I'm thirsty," I said when the girls came out in their regular clothes, carrying several dresses they were buying. "Let's take a shopping break for snacks and drinks."

"Deal!" Amelia said, as Hunter took the clothes and handbag from her to go pay for them. "There's that Mexican food place just around the corner from here that has amazing nachos and delicious margaritas."

"You had me at nachos," Erina said.

"We should get a pitcher of margaritas," I suggested as I followed Erina up to the counter.

"It's like you're reading my mind," Amelia said. She picked up a shiny bracelet from the counter display and tossed it on top of the clothes pile.

Hunter's lips twitched, but he made no comment.

I found it hilarious to see her buy cheap costume jewelry when Stephan and her other husbands were billionaires who constantly purchased her million-dollar diamonds. Perhaps, that's what made her so happy, enjoying the simple things in life even while being a billionaire. Maybe I needed to try it?

I looked at the jewelry and grabbed a pink rhinestone bracelet, there was a green one and a blue one as well. "Matching bracelets?" I asked aloud.

"Dibs on green!" Erina said and grabbed that one.

"Pink or blue?" Amelia asked me. "You know I like either."

"I'll take pink since it'll remind me of you," I said.

She set the blue one next to the other bracelet. "Blue will remind me of you, too. You always look the best in blue."

Once we bought the bracelets, we all put them on and walked side by side to the Mexican food restaurant. For the first time in my life, I stood in line with average people, waiting for my turn.

"I don't think I've waited in line since I was a teenager," Erina whispered.

I chuckled. "I was just thinking that."

"Haughty bitches," Amelia teased with a smile. "It's nice to live like a normal person from time to time. Reminds me of how far I've come, and allows me to enjoy the finer things in life more."

"I think I need to take tips from you to live a happier life," I commented.

Her eyes widened and she stared at me in silence for a long blink. "Really?"

I nodded. "Seriously. You're always so happy, and you're right, there are often times that I forget to enjoy the niceties I have now because I've become used to it, but if you hadn't saved Brian, I might not have them in the future."

Amelia frowned. "I keep forgetting that you two grew up in mafia households before you met your husbands."

Patting her shoulder, I said, "It's understandable for someone who came from outside not to know what it was like to grow up in a house of one. It's sort of funny when you think about it."

"What is?" Erina asked.

"If Stanley had known about Amelia, she might have grown up in a mafia household too, and who knows how she would have turned out then."

"Mom raised me to handle weapons and Randolph trained me for research, so I guess I was raised mafia-lite?" She tapped her chin. "That's an interesting topic to bring up next time I see my mom."

"Can I please be present for that discussion?" Erina begged.

My attempt to hold back my laughter failed and I laughed loudly.

"I'm serious," Erina said.

"I know. I was just thinking how interesting it's going to be to witness Amelia's mother trying to explain why she trained Amelia the way she did, and you said that, so it was funny to me," I explained.

"Please follow me," a petite woman with thick, wavy hair, wearing a low-cut shirt with skintight jeans, and sporting a lovely figure told us.

We followed, going into a large room with a lot of people and a lot of noise. It didn't really bother me, but it was definitely a different atmosphere than the one I was used to.

I was immediately struck by the vibrant colors and festive decor. The walls were painted in warm shades of red, yellow, and orange, with intricate tile work lining the bar area.

As I made my way to the table, I couldn't help but notice the spices and herbs wafting through the air. It was a tantalizing mix of cumin, chili powder, and fresh cilantro.

Once seated, I took a moment to appreciate the colorful tablecloth and the ceramic plates and utensils. It was a little odd to be sitting on a metal chair, a little cold on my butt, but not awful.

It was the first time I'd had to scoot in my own chair.

At that thought, I mentally chastised myself. This was how spoiled I was! Amelia was right, I needed to do more normal things more often, to reflect on how ridiculous I had become.

I didn't bother looking at the menu because we had

decided ahead of time on what we were getting, and Amelia always liked to order for us.

The waiter came over, a handsome young man with large biceps on display. He smiled, showing off twin dimples. "Good evening. Can I get you lovely ladies started with something to drink?"

"We'd like a margarita pitcher," Amelia ordered. "The house margarita. Two glasses with salt and one without." She looked at Hunter. "You want to share the margarita with us?"

He shook his head. "No, I'll have the local amber beer I saw on tap."

The waiter nodded and smiled at Hunter. "That's a great choice. That beer is delicious."

"I've never had it, but I'll give it a try," Hunter said.

"I always say you have to try everything once," the waiter said and winked at Hunter.

His cheeks reddened as I think he realized that the man was flirting with him.

"We're actually ready to order food, too. We want the nachos appetizer with chicken, and put the guacamole on the side. Also, extra sour cream on the side, too."

She ordered the food like it was something she did all the time.

Was it?

Once he left to put in our order, I asked.

She shook her head. "I used to order that a lot before I met my husbands, but I haven't gone out like this since then." She smiled wide. "Sometimes it's nice, you know, going back to your roots. I spent many a drunken night eating nachos at restaurants similar to this."

"Did you have many female friends before?" Erina asked.

Amelia shook her head. "No, actually. I had one friend for a bit, but we were just too different. You two are my first female best friends."

"And only," I said with a serious look that only lasted four seconds before the three of us burst into laughter.

"What about you two?" Amelia asked.

"I didn't really have friends aside from Brian before you two," I admitted. As soon as I said it, I felt embarrassed, but I ignored the embarrassment.

"Same," Erina said. "I tried to make friends with some of the officers' wives, but they just didn't click with me. Not like you two."

"Well, I guess it's a good thing," Amelia said.

"How so?" I asked.

She smiled wide. "If you'd found your best female friends before, you wouldn't have been willing to become my best friends."

Erina and I laughed softly and I shook my head at her. But ... maybe she was right.

The margarita pitcher arrived and Hunter poured the glasses for us. Once everyone had a drink, Amelia raised hers up over the center of the table. "To best friends."

"Best friends," Erina and I said and clinked our glasses against each other's.

Amelia pouted. "Hunter, you're supposed to do cheers with us."

He clinked his glass against hers and smiled. "Cheers."

She smiled again and started looking around while drinking from her glass.

I took a hesitant sip of mine, but it turned out to be pretty good. Not the best tequila I'd ever had, but still tasty. Following Amelia's lead, I started looking around as well.

As I looked around the Mexican restaurant, I took in the diverse patrons enjoying their meals. There were families with young children, couples on romantic dates, and groups of friends gathered together for a night out. At one table, a family of four laughed and joked as they passed around a basket of tortilla chips and salsa. The parents shared their entrees with their children. At another table, a couple was enjoying a meal together, sharing a pitcher of margaritas and a plate of sizzling fajitas. They seemed lost in their own world, completely absorbed in each other's company. Further back, a group of five female friends celebrated a birthday, singing and clapping along to the restaurant employee's wishing one of them a happy birthday. Despite the differences in age and background, everyone in the restaurant seemed to be having a great time, chatting and laughing as they enjoyed the flavorful dishes and each other's company. The lively atmosphere of the restaurant seemed to bring everyone together, creating a sense of community and warmth.

For the first time in a very long time, I actually felt happy and at peace. Surrounded by average people, all enjoying the same foods, sights, and sounds. Amelia was right, I needed to do this more often.

The food arrived and we eagerly dug in. The nacho cheese, crispy chips, flavorful chicken, and spicy salsa made for the perfect meal.

"Remind me to do this more often," Erina said around a mouthful of food. "So good."

I nodded my agreement. "Was just thinking that."

"We can set up friend dates where I take you to all the best, cheap restaurants," Amelia said with excitement. "Have you ever been to a Benihana's?"

"A Beni-what?" I asked.

She laughed. "Perfect! That can be our first one."

Hunter's phone chimed at the same time that Amelia's did.

Erina's phone rang immediately afterwards, as did mine.

What was happening?

Chapter 17

Amelia

I opened my phone to read the text message, when it rang with a call from Stephan.

"Hello?" I answered.

Erin and Marlee got phone calls as well.

"Someone blew up our building," Stephan said. "Thankfully, the staff were evacuated beforehand."

"What! Someone blew up our house!" Erina.

"Our house ... exploded?" Marlee gasped.

I hung up with Stephan, not bothering with pleasantries, and dialed my mother, standing and pacing as I waited for her to answer.

"Aren't you supposed to—"

"Get out of the house!" I screamed.

All of the people inside the restaurant had turned to look at our table, but I didn't care. All I cared about was my mom and the babies getting to safety.

She hung up, which I hoped meant she was grabbing the babies and escaping.

I called Stephan back. "I told Mom to evacuate. Marlee and Erina's houses got blown up, too."

"Shit, I'm glad you're with them. I thought he'd just destroyed our business as his failsafe," he said and sighed. "Did she get out?"

"I don't know. She hung up when I told her to evacuate. Can you check the surveillance cameras?"

"Checking now," Dane said, making it clear Stephan had put me on speakerphone.

"Everything's down, but there is video from two minutes ago showing your mom, Randolph, and the babies running away from the house," Dane said after a moment of silence.

Mom started calling me. "She's calling me."

"Conference her in," Stephan ordered me.

I answered the call and then added her to the first call. "Mom? You okay?"

"We got out in time," she said, huffing and puffing. "Damn, I need to do cardio more."

"Both babies are safe," Randolph said as he took over talking, probably taking the phone from Mom so she could wrangle the babies and catch her breath. "Your house is destroyed. We're in the car headed to the nearest safe house."

I fell into my seat and Hunter reached out a hand to steady me and keep me from falling over. "Thank goodness."

"You really pissed off Collman, huh?" Randolph asked.

"I shot him in the face," I said softly. "Twice."

"This was likely his failsafe for if he died," Stephan said. "One last f-you to us. He blew up our building downtown, too."

"Marlee? Erina?" I asked. "Was it just your houses? Is everyone okay?"

"He blew up our hotel that was in development," Marlee said softly, tears in her eyes. "That son of a bitch."

"I can't reach Jasper," Erina said softly. "I don't know if he made it out."

Marlee reached over and grasped her hand. "I'm sure he made it out. He's a wily, old man."

Jasper was Erina's butler, someone she'd known for decades and loved and trusted. He was a kind, old man and I hoped he was okay.

"What are we going to do? All of our houses are destroyed," I whispered.

"Come back to the hotel," Stephan said. "We'll discuss it more when you're here."

"Okay," I agreed sadly. I'd spent a lot of time and effort on that house. I'd had irreplaceable items there. Mementos from our trips, things I couldn't just buy again.

Hunter gave the waiter a wad of cash and got us all out of our seats and headed back to the hotel.

We silently walked through the crowds, ignoring the hawkers and people trying to get us to take photos with them for money.

In two minutes, we'd all lost so much, and it made us all feel a bit numb.

Erina's phone rang and she immediately answered. "Jasper?" She exhaled harshly. "Oh, thank goodness you're alright. Yes, I'm safe, too. Call Connor and see where he wants you to go. I'm so glad you're okay, Jasper. Yes. Yes. Okay."

She hung up and I squeezed one of her hands with a smile.

Erina and Marlee held hands as they rode the elevator with Hunter and I in front of them.

I leaned my head against Hunter's shoulder. "I should have made him suffer."

He put his arm around my shoulders and squeezed. "What's important is that no one was hurt."

"Right," I agreed.

Inside the penthouse suite, we found Brian, all of Erina's husbands, and all of mine as well gathered together in the living room.

Erina sat on Connor's lap on the couch, burying her face into his neck as he spoke to someone, likely Jasper, on the phone.

Marlee sat next to Brian and he put his arm around her shoulders.

Shea patted his lap and I immediately sat on it, letting him wrap his large arms around me. "It's okay," he whispered in my ear. "Everyone's okay."

"Our house," I whined. "Our beautiful house."

"We'll build a new one," he promised. "An even better one."

"Where are we going to stay?" Marlee asked Brian softly. "He blew up the hotel, too."

"We can stay at one of our hotels downtown for a while," Brian replied.

An idea struck me and I leaned over, tapping Stephan's shoulder to get his attention.

He turned and smiled at me, ran his knuckles down my cheek, and asked, "What is it, darling?"

"What if we all went to the beach house?" I suggested.

"The beach house?" he asked.

I nodded and looked at Marlee and Erina. "I think we all deserve a little vacation, and our beach house is really a resort, not a house. We have enough rooms for everyone here, plus a dozen more people. Erina could bring Jasper. My mom and Randolph could come. There's even a daycare area where we could play with the kids. We could all spend time relaxing at the beach while getting our houses rebuilt or buying new ones."

"That sounds amazing," Marlee said and looked at Brian.

He set his hand on her cheek, smiled, and said, "Whatever you want, my love. If you want to spend more time with Amelia, and Stephan is willing to let us crash there, then that's what we'll do."

I looked back at Stephan, who hadn't stopped smiling. "You know I can't say no to you. What do you say, Connor? Fancy a beach vacation?"

Connor silently stared at the floor, his fingers tapping on his knee.

"The answer is yes, we do fancy a beach vacation, especially one with my friends who will keep me from going stir crazy, because I know he's going to get super protective after this," Erina said.

Connor raised his head and she narrowed her eyes. His scowl turned into a smile. "I was going to say that sounds nice, but you beat me to it."

Her eyes widened. "You mean it?"

Connor looked over at me. "Amelia has more than proven that she's trustworthy. Not only in protecting you, but she saved Brian today and rescued us all. So, if you can learn to trust her and her husbands, then so can I."

Erina's mouth dropped and she threw her arms around his neck. "I knew it wasn't too late to teach this old dog new tricks."

"Hey!" Connor protested.

Everyone, myself included, laughed at the couple.

"So, we're in agreement?" I asked. "We're going to go to the beach, drink while soaking up the sun, and help each other design or find our new houses?"

"Sounds awesome," Shea said, nuzzling my hair.

"Let me call and get things in motion," Stephan said, and headed into the other room.

"Should I call Mom?" I asked Shea.

"On it," Dane said and held up his phone that showed he was already calling her as he walked to the patio.

"Did you have a good day today? Aside from the house being blown up?" Brian asked Marlee.

She nodded. "Amelia took me to a Mexican restaurant and made me stand in line like a normal person."

"How quaint," Brian teased.

"We sat on cold metal chairs, and I realized how spoiled I am because it was the first time I've had to scoot my own chair in at a restaurant since we started dating."

He chuckled and kissed the side of her head. "Sounds awful. I'm so sorry I wasn't there to push your chair in for you."

"No, actually, it made me realize just how spoiled I am."

She frowned. "Maybe it's good timing. Maybe it'll be better for me to remember this when we're deciding on the next house. I'm not saying I'm going to give up all my niceties, but I'll be a little less picky about certain things and a little more reserved."

"So, not only is she offering you a beach vacation, but she allowed you to have an epiphany today?" Brian asked.

"And saved your life yesterday," she reminded him.

"Sounds like we better get her something really nice for her birthday," he said with a wink at me.

"Monthly girls' outings without objection would be a nice present," I replied with a wide smile.

"I'll think about it," he said.

"Next time I'll save you last," I threatened.

Marlee laughed and shook her head. "Don't think that's an idle threat either, love. She means it. She'll let you sweat while she rescues the rest of them first."

"As long as she saves you first, that's all that matters," Brian said.

"Aw," I said. I put my hands together, and tilted my face against them like I was looking at the cutest puppy. "You're so sweet." I looked back at Shea. "You used to say nice things like that, too."

He rolled his eyes. "I'm so sorry I haven't said anything nice in the past two days, but you haven't even been with me."

"You could have said something nice when I rescued you. Arcadio praised me and gave me a good kiss."

"Arcadio's crazy, so that's not really fair," Shea countered.

"Crazy about my goddess," Arcadio said behind me.

I turned and he kissed my lips lightly. "Bonus points to Arcadio."

Shea grumbled and shoved me off his lap. "Fine, go sit on the cold couch."

Erina and Marlee doubled over in laughter.

Erina slapped Connor's shoulder. "See! I told you! They're always like this."

Stephan came back and took a moment to look around the room. "I clearly missed something."

"Shea's being mean to me." I stuck my lip out in a pout.

Stephan smiled and took his seat beside Shea again. "Shea's usually the nicest. Perhaps he's been taking tips from Dane."

"Hey!" Dane shouted from the other room. "I heard that."

"I think Shea's jealous, because Hunter is better than him at pretty much every game and you spend more time playing with Hunter than him," Arcadio said.

"Get good," I said with an unapologetic shrug.

Blain let out a bark of laughter before covering his mouth with his hand.

"One v one," Shea challenged Hunter.

My mouth dropped and I said, "My consoles! All of my data and consoles are gone! That asshole destroyed months of gaming data. God dammit! All of my games!"

"We can buy the games again," Stephan reminded me.

"Your saved data should have been uploaded to the cloud," Hunter said. "I think all of our data is safe."

"I hope so. I don't want to have to go back through all those matches again with newbies who can't even follow simple directions." I huffed and crossed my arms over my chest. Another realization hit me. "Wait, you don't have suits!" I looked at Stephan and smiled wide.

"Why are you so happy I lost my suits?" he asked with a frown.

"Because that means we can't go to the fundraiser! I don't have to go to that boring fundraiser with you!" Standing up, I danced in a circle in front of the couch.

"Oh, I can just buy one at the store down the street. They have tailored suits for me before, and have my measurements on file," Stephan said with a smile.

"Uh, but I don't have a dress," I said.

"We bought one today, remember?" Marlee reminded me helpfully.

"Oh, right. Thank you for reminding me." My voice was strained, as was my smile, which only made her smile wider.

"Perhaps our friends here would like to go to the fundraiser as well?" Stephan suggested. "I know your friends wouldn't want you to be bored and lonely."

An evil smile spread across my face. He was totally setting them up to have to go with me. "Yes, I think you're right. Our friends should definitely come with us. It can be their payment for staying at the beach resort."

"I changed my mind," Marlee said, "I don't want to go to the beach."

Stephan and Brian laughed.

"Connor," Erina whined. "Don't make me go."

"Oh, it's about time you got back into high society, darling." He kissed her cheek. "This is a perfect opportunity."

Erina glared at me. "You'll pay for this."

"We'll get her back when we are at the beach resort," Marlee said to Erina.

"Hey! No scheming!" I yelled.

"Darling, that's what we do best," Erina said with a bright smile.

"Now I've changed *my* mind. I don't want them coming to our beach resort. Let them live in a boring hotel in the middle of downtown," I said and folded my arms across my chest. "No drinks with umbrellas provided by sexy men in speedos for you two."

"Where are you getting these sexy men?" Shea asked.

"I know people," I said with a nonchalant shrug of one shoulder and looked at my fingernails.

Shea grabbed me and pulled me down onto his lap. "Are you trying to get a rise out of me, wife?"

"Ew, we're sitting right here," Erina said. "No talking about anything rising, okay?"

"Children, behave," Stephan threatened Shea and I.

I stuck my tongue out at Erina, and she did it in return.

Chapter 18

Erina

Laying on a lounge chair on the beach with sunshine warming my skin, listening to the waves crashing against the shore, the scent of salt in the air, and the sound of my friends and family laughing nearby was definitely my favorite place. It was made even better by the sweet, fruity drink with a blue umbrella and a matching blue swirly straw I was currently sipping on.

Amelia and Marlee lay on either side of me. Marlee wore a cute, white, one-piece bathing suit with a gold chain around her waist, a giant white hat, and sunglasses. She was seated upright to drink her Mai Tai more easily and hadn't stopped smiling since we arrived.

Amelia wore a dark blue bikini and had her husbands coming over every forty minutes to make her turn over and apply more sunscreen to keep her from burning. She'd just finished her drink and raised the empty glass into the air. "Cabana Boy!" she called out.

I had no idea how they'd decided who was going to be her

designated "cabana boy" today, but Arcadio wore nothing but a tight speedo, his wavy black hair tied up in a bun so the wind wouldn't blow it around. He strutted over, fully aware of his sex appeal, and knelt on one knee next to her. "You called, my goddess?"

"We need another round," she informed him. "And some snacks."

"Would you like me to feed you the snacks, or would you like some that you can feed yourself?" he asked.

"Feed myself," she said. "I think my friends might throw up our drinks if they witness just how adorable we are together."

I rolled my eyes, but couldn't stop the smile that spread on my face. They really were all adorable together. I'd thought that my husbands and I were an anomaly, but their group got along really well together, too.

"As you wish," he said. He stood, bowed, and gathered our glasses.

"This is so much better than any other beach vacation I've taken before," Marlee said with a content sigh.

"Same," I agreed with a nod.

"Do you think this is what Collman envisioned when he set it up to blow up our houses?" Amelia asked with a snicker. "I wish I could see his face as he witnessed us bonding even more and thoroughly enjoying ourselves."

It sucked to lose our houses, but she was right. Collman would likely have been furious to know that his plan to demoralize us by blowing our shit up hadn't worked.

Instead of being depressed, I was enjoying one of the best vacations of my life.

"Can we make this an annual trip?" I asked. "I know the kids would continue to enjoy coming here as they get older and I certainly won't mind being here a week each summer."

"Sounds like a great plan to me," Marlee said. "Although, this has made me want to look at buying my own resort on one of the islands off the southeast. Maybe we could rotate the trips around to our different locations?"

"Oh, I like that idea," Amelia said. "Then it won't get repetitive or boring, since we'd only come here once every three years."

"Deal," I said. "I'll start looking for places for Connor to buy after we've got the new house built."

"Are you going to rebuild or move?" Amelia asked Marlee.

It was something that she and Brian and been discussing, not very quietly, for several days. A few times, I'd considered interrupting them to stop them from shouting so much, but remembered that I wasn't exactly quiet when talking about something I was passionate about with my husbands, either.

Marlee sighed. "We've been arguing about it for days. He's so damn stubborn."

I made no comment, agreeing that we knew. See, I was learning how to behave.

"Ultimately, we agreed to move. Clearly, our location was known by enemies and even if Angel Eyes is gone, that doesn't mean that people he was affiliated with won't retaliate or continue their aggression in hopes of taking over our territory."

"That's a good point," Amelia agreed. "I know we want to build a new house, but now I'm wondering if we need to find new land as well." She tapped a finger against the lounge she lay on as she considered it.

"What about you?" Marlee asked me.

"We're moving and building new," I answered. We, like my friends, had spent several days discussing it. We'd drawn up pros and cons, suggested some areas we knew of, and Damien had even started drawing up ideas for things he wanted in the house. I told him I wanted my own secret room that doubled as a panic room for both my mental and potentially physical health. Connor had immediately agreed with the idea, but insisted that we include a secret passageway to connect Melina's room to that room as well in case she needed a panic room.

"Too bad we couldn't just buy a commune and live together," Amelia muttered as she continued tapping.

I laughed and shook my head. "I love you two, and while this is a great vacation, I need some space as well."

"Distance makes the heart grow fonder," Marlee agreed. "It will make our times together even sweeter."

"Sure. Sure," Amelia said, clearly only half listening as she contemplated her plans and likely was drawing up schemes of some sort that her husbands would groan about, but ultimately agree to, later.

We became silent, listening to the ocean and lost in our own minds. Even silently sitting together contemplating things was nice when with them.

"Your drinks, dear goddesses," Arcadio said as he carried a tray over to us. He divvied out the drinks, giving Amelia a kiss on the cheek as he handed her hers.

Dane and Forrest walked over. Dane set a small table

between Marlee and I while Forrest set an identical table between me and Amelia.

Shea came out shortly after Dane and Forrest returned to their chairs on the patio. He carried a large tray with two platters of food and set one on each of the tables. "Your snacks have been prepared and we hope you enjoy the assortment."

I eagerly picked up a piece of crispy fried chicken, the crunch of the coating giving way to the juicy meat inside. The savory flavor was perfectly balanced with a hint of spice, making my taste buds tingle with pleasure. Next, I reached for a handful of freshly baked garlic breadsticks, their warm aroma wafting up to greet me. The bread was soft and fluffy, with a buttery garlic flavor that melted in my mouth. As I continued to graze, I tried the tangy pickles and olives, their briny taste a refreshing break from the rich flavors of the other snacks. The plate of fresh fruit, including plump strawberries and juicy watermelon slices, provided a sweet and refreshing finish to my snacking session. Overall, the tray of food was a perfect combination of flavors and textures, leaving me feeling satisfied and content.

"This is why she doesn't want a chef," Marlee commented as she licked her fingers clean. "Her men cook well enough that it doesn't warrant it."

Amelia chuckled. "I'll be sure to pass your compliments on to them. The issue we have is that we end up so busy that no one has the time to cook."

Hunter walked out wearing a pair of short shorts, showing off his incredibly muscular body as well as a few scars, one from when he'd gotten shot protecting us. Forrest and Dane teased him about something, but Hunter just flipped them off and headed into the water.

"You can't have him," Amelia said. "He's my bodyguard and I don't want to replace him."

I rolled my eyes at her. "I don't want any additional men, thank you. However, I am allowed to look, you know? You're as bad as Connor. Every time he sees me looking at a man, he tells me I can't add him to my harem. What's the point of having eyes if I don't use them to enjoy the beauty around us?"

I could have admitted that I was looking at the scar and thinking about how lucky we were to have had him with us during our escape and rescue, but that would have brought Amelia's mood down and I wouldn't do anything to sour it.

"He is incredibly ripped," Marlee commented. "I'm surprised that he hasn't put on some fluff now that he's not actively fighting."

"I asked him about that, actually," Amelia admitted. "He said, 'old habits die hard,' as if that explained why he was counting calories. I tried deleting his app, but he said it didn't matter because he has the calorie counts memorized for the foods he eats. Stephan said to give him six more months and if he doesn't start adjusting, that he'll talk to him and see about possibly suggesting counseling."

"You think it's become an eating disorder?" Marlee asked.

Amelia shook her head. "I don't think so, but Stephan said it's better to be safe than sorry, and even if it's not a disorder, there's a lot of trauma he's been dealing with that a counselor could help him with."

"I need to find one again," I said with a groan. "It's been a long time and I know I've let a lot of things go on too long."

"It's hard to talk to a therapist when you can't admit that you're a mafia wife," Marlee said. "I stopped going because I found it too difficult."

Amelia nodded. "It is difficult. We have one on staff if you'd like her information. She's fully licensed and everything would be one hundred percent confidential. She takes it very seriously. Her dad was part of our family, and she offered her services once she got her license. Stephan pays her very well for her service and confidentiality."

"I'd like her info," Marlee said. "Please."

"Me, too," I seconded.

"I'll send it to you this evening. Remind me tomorrow if I forget."

"Let's go get in the water," I suggested and stood. "We should work off a little of that delicious food we just ate."

Amelia stood and stretched with a squeal. "I was getting too warm, so the cool water sounds like a great idea."

"Well, if you're both going I guess I can't stay here by myself," Marlee said with a sigh. "You young women are going to be the death of me."

"Come on, granny," Amelia teased.

Marlee tossed her hat off and glared. "Oh, you're going to get it."

Amelia pushed her nose up and made a silly face at Marlee, who immediately ran after her, forcing Amelia to run towards the water.

Chapter 19

Stephan

I sat on the beach with my feet in the sand, watching Amelia, Marlee, and Erina play in the ocean. The sun beat down on my skin, warming me up as I sat and enjoyed the scenery. Amelia was in the water, laughing and splashing around with her friends. They looked like they were having the time of their lives, and I couldn't help but smile as I watched them.

I didn't mind sitting on the beach and watching from afar. I liked the ocean, but I didn't really enjoy swimming in it. I preferred to stay on dry land. Watching my wife play in the ocean was more enjoyable for me. As I sat there, I couldn't help but think about how lucky I was to have her in my life. She was beautiful, smart, and funny, and she always knew how to make me smile. Watching her play in the ocean with her friends was a reminder of how much fun she could be. I loved seeing her happy and carefree, and I knew that being around her was what made me the happiest.

Seeing her walk into the conference room, shotgun blasting, had been both terrifying and amazing at the same time.

She always surprised me with how she handled situations, and her handling of Santino Collman had been eye opening. Her quick thinking and wit had literally saved our lives, not to mention her quick dagger throw that had saved Brian.

The fact that the bastard had blown up our buildings and houses infuriated me so much that I wished I could bring him back to life so I could kill him with my own hands. I should have found him and killed him as soon as he offered to buy Amelia, but I'd tried to keep my jealousy and anger at bay. Had I done it, we all would have suffered far less.

"It's nice seeing her smile," Brian said as he sat in a chair beside me. I knew he meant his wife, so I didn't bother asking. "She really enjoys being around Amelia."

"I don't know many people who *don't* enjoy being around her," I said with a proud smile.

"She is quite the character," Connor said as he joined us. "I'm honestly surprised to see you with a woman like her, though. She's definitely not someone I would have picked for you."

"Good thing you didn't pick then. I would have been sorely disappointed," I teased.

Sitting at my beach resort, with a fellow mafia boss on either side of me, their families playing in the sand beside me with my family, was surreal. Five years ago, I would have laughed if anyone had suggested this could happen.

Yet, my wife had a way of bringing people together. That's why she fit with me and my brothers so well.

"Have you decided where you're going to buy yet?" Connor asked Brian.

Brian sighed and shook his head. "No, we've been going over our options for days."

"We all heard," Connor said.

I shook my head at the man who could have kept that part to himself, but his social graces were a bit lacking.

"Sorry about that," Brian muttered. He looked over at his wife and said, "I want her to be safe, but it's hard to admit when I'm wrong."

"Preaching to the choir on that one," Connor said and chuckled softly.

We all watched our wives in silence, enjoying their laughs.

"We're looking at property in the valley," I said. "It reminds Amelia of her childhood and having a lot of open, flat land will allow us to build multiple houses for her mother to move into, as well as give Hunter his own place so he doesn't feel so awkward."

"I still need to fight him," Connor said.

"You do not need to fight my wife's bodyguard," I said, despite the smile on my face.

"Erina keeps talking about how he tossed a guy on the ground and got him into an arm bar faster than she's ever seen anyone move before. I know she's just telling me about it because she witnessed it while he was protecting her, but I also feel like it's a challenge," Connor explained.

Hunter had gone above and beyond in the past week, and was going to get a very nice bonus as thanks.

"How long does it take for fighters to stop focusing on eating habits?" I asked Connor.

"It varies, obviously, but a few months," he answered

immediately. He looked back over at Hunter. "That's why he's so ripped? He's still counting calories and eating like he's prepping for fights?"

I nodded. "Amelia tried to delete his app, but he has the calories memorized and it's hard to get him to deviate from set meals."

"To be fair, if he hadn't been in prime fighting shape, he might not have been able to protect the girls as well as he did this week," Connor said.

"I know, but I don't want him to be so stressed about it," I explained. "He can be in fighting shape without depriving himself of good food."

"You want me to talk to him?" Connor asked.

"I was thinking more like asking Blain to talk to him," I explained.

Connor nodded. "I'll mention it to him. We'll be here a few more days at least, so he can find time to work it in naturally. I know Hunter's been spending a lot of time with the guys."

"I'm surprised you let her get a guard outside of your group," Brian commented. "What if she'd decided she wanted to add him on as a sixth?"

"We have a very good, open line of communication in our marriage group," I said calmly. It wasn't abnormal for people to question our relationship, and I expected it from Brian since he witnessed it with both Connor and I. "Hunter is like a brother to her, so I don't have to worry about it."

"Do you think Collman left any other surprises for us?" Brian asked.

We stewed in silence a moment before Connor broke it.

"If he did, we'll handle it. Now that the bastard is dead, whatever surprises he left won't mean shit. My men found the ones who'd planted the bombs at our house and building and they've been dealt with."

"We found one of the groups," I said, "but the ones who planted them at our house are still missing. It shouldn't be too long before they're found, though. I put a high price on their heads. Even their friends will consider selling them out."

"Have your men questioned the ones who've been caught?" Brian asked.

"They haven't gotten much from them," Connor said with a grunt. "They claim they were paid to plant the bombs and that they received a text from an unknown number."

"The ones we captured said the same thing," I said, clenching my fists. "They don't know if it was Collman who sent it or someone who'd been under him. I suppose it would have been easy to pay someone to send out texts if he didn't check in at a certain time."

"The sooner we eradicate them, the better I'll feel," Brian said. "I don't like constantly looking over my shoulder."

"We'll find them all," I said with certainty.

"And we'll make others see exactly what happens when you cross us," Connor said. "No one will mess with us after they see what we do."

On that, we could all agree.

As the sun began to set and a cold breeze started blowing, Amelia, Marlee, and Erina finally made their way back to shore. Amelia came over to me, her skin glistening with water, and gave me a kiss on the cheek.

"Having a good time?" she asked.

"Of course," I replied, still watching her with adoration. "I had a great time just watching you have fun."

Erina sat on Connor's lap and rubbed her wet face against his. "Did you miss me?"

"Ugh, you're so cold!" Connor complained. He picked her up and carried her to the patio, where Alexi was ready with a towel.

"You two getting along?" Marlee asked and leaned against Brian's chair.

"He's been utterly horrible to me," I lied.

Marlee smacked his arm. "Brian!"

My head fell back as I laughed.

"He's lying," Brian said and grabbed her hands. "We've been getting along great. Until now, bastard."

Amelia grabbed my hand and tugged. "Let's go inside and have dinner. It's too chilly out here tonight."

"Yes, ma'am," I said and stood obediently.

"What's for dinner?" Marlee asked as she walked beside Amelia up the steps.

"Thank you," Brian said softly as we stood alone on the beach watching everyone head inside.

"For what?" I asked, and turned to face him.

"Everything. You've given my wife a friend, helped us several times, and encouraged our alliance and, dare I say, friendship. I'm a stubborn, egotistical, prick quite often and if it weren't for you, I'm not sure what would have happened."

I set my hand on his shoulder and smiled. "That's what friends are for, Brian. Plus, most of that was my wife's work."

"True, but you could have told her she was crazy and refused to do all the things," he countered.

I laughed and shook my head. "Have you met my wife? You think I can tell her anything?"

He laughed with me and we headed inside.

It was nice having friends, especially ones that understood the pressures and complications of running both legitimate businesses and mafia ones. Honestly, I was the thankful one even if I wouldn't say it out loud just yet.

We headed towards the sound of laughter, and found everyone in the giant dining room.

Amelia was seated at the head of the table, a place she didn't normally take, but I was certain she hadn't even realized she had gone to. She was most often the center of attention, though she didn't realize it.

Her bright, beautiful aura attracted everyone. I was so glad we had snatched her up when we did.

"Everything okay?" Shea asked me.

I nodded. "Just enjoying seeing her laugh and smile with her friends."

"It does make me feel good," Shea said. "She brightens up every room she walks into, but when she's with those two, she's almost too bright to look at."

"On that, we are in agreeance," I said.

I was going to do everything in my power to ensure she was kept safe. We were going to exterminate every person who wanted to do her harm. Especially, the ones who had blown up our house and business. If she had been there ... If our children had been there ...

I couldn't even think about that without becoming upset.

"Increase the price on their heads," I whispered to Shea. "I want them found as soon as possible and buried."

Shea's eyes widened. "Interrogated first?"

"Quickly. I don't want them to have the chance to escape," I explained.

His brows drew together, but he nodded and said, "I'll do that right now."

I grabbed his forearm as he tried to walk away. "After dinner. She'll notice that you're gone and ask questions."

"Okay," he agreed and walked to an open seat next to Amelia.

One final open seat was available, at her right hand side. I took that place and she immediately set her hand on mine on top of the table as she continued talking to Erina, telling her about something that Paige had done.

As I sat beside her, I wanted to squeeze her, but I restrained myself, instead just listening to her and laughing along with everyone else.

I was one of the luckiest men in the world, and I would do everything in my power to ensure that I could keep her safe, so our lives would continue being amazing.

Chapter 20

Erina

Staying at the beach resort with everyone was a dream vacation I hadn't even realized I had dreamed of.

There were no cooks, servants, or staff of any kind. Instead, we all took turns cooking, making snacks, doing dishes, and washing laundry.

Most often, Amelia was doing them even when it wasn't her turn. She said it was habit from her life at home, and that it made her feel useful when she wasn't able to work.

Today, it was my turn to wash clothes and Amelia was right beside me, helping to separate and fold it all.

"Is this what it's like for you at home?" I asked.

She nodded. "Well, except that instead of it being you, it would be one of my husbands."

"Oh? Am I not manly enough for you?" I teased.

She snickered. "Oftentimes, they use helping me do chores as a way to take a break from a problem at work that they can't solve. They'll talk to me about whatever the issue is and what solutions they're considering, or how they can't come up with a solution. Most of the time, I just listen, making sounds of understanding, even if I don't, and they end up answering their own questions. Other times, I will offer suggestions or ask more questions to get them to think about it from another perspective. They do the same for me when I have an issue."

"That sounds lovely," I admitted. My husbands listened when I had problems and tried to help, but I never thought about how cathartic it would be to have a daily option to walk away from your desk, help with something that also needed to get done, and find a solution to your problem. "You guys really do work well together."

"It's not all sunshine and rainbows," she muttered as she folded a pair of socks together. "We argue and get our feelings hurt still. There are times I have to remind them that I do not in fact have a favorite, and that if I was spending more time with that person than the others, it wasn't on purpose or to upset the others. I'm fairly certain they made a calendar to help prevent those issues, though I haven't been able to find said calendar."

After scanning our surroundings to make sure no one was nearby, I said, "Our biggest issues is sex."

"Like, how often you have it or making sure you're being equal?" she asked softly.

This was one of the reasons I was so glad to have her as a friend. She understood the trials and tribulations of being with multiple men.

"Keeping it equal," I replied. "It's hard when some of them are more aggressive and a few are reserved. Damien won't push for it, so if I'm not careful, we might go two weeks or more without being together. Alexi is often away at missions, so when he is home, we take advantage of that time and he's very aggressive in his desires and won't restrain himself from walking into the room, grabbing me, and throwing me over his shoulder. It's not that I prefer sex with Alexi versus Damien, they're very different types of lovers, but sometimes it's easier to just allow the aggressive ones to lead, and I forget to take into account Damien's feelings and personality."

Amelia nodded. "I have the same issue with Shea and Arcadio."

"Shea's the gentle giant, isn't he?" I asked with a small smile.

She nodded again. "And like Alexi, Arcadio is often gone on missions, so he's very aggressive with his desires when he is home."

"What about Stephan?" I asked curiously.

She froze; her entire body went rigid and it didn't look like she was breathing.

"Amelia?" I asked softly. She still didn't move. "You don't have to tell me about it if you don't want." We talked about everything, so her sudden quietness concerned me. Was he abusive? I couldn't see Stephan being abusive, but then again, that was how most abusers stayed hidden.

"I'll be right back," she said and left the laundry room.

I continued folding shirts and pants, my brows furrowed in concern. If Stephan was abusive, it would be very hard to get her away from him. As the boss, he had a lot of power over the others. But after seeing them all together for so long, I found it hard to believe that her loving and adoring men would let anyone harm her, even their boss.

If he was abusive though, I would do everything in my power to help her break free.

She came back, shut the door behind her, and said, "Sorry. I had to check with Stephan before I talked to you since it's not my right to share his secrets."

My brows rose and I blinked in silence. "Okay?"

"Stephan's asexual," she blurted. "He has romantic feelings, but not sexual ones. He does like hand holding and cuddling, but we don't fool around or have sex."

My jaw dropped figuratively and literally at her admission. I'd noticed that he wasn't as affectionate as the others towards her, but assumed he was just more reserved, like Brian was with Marlee. This was definitely not what I had thought was the actual reason.

She looked at me expectantly.

I threw arms around her and groaned. "Thank fuck. I thought you froze because he was abusive and was trying to figure out how I was going to rescue you from the marriage."

She laughed, then pushed me back, saw I was serious, hugged me tightly, and then doubled over in laughter, falling onto the floor as she held her stomach.

"That explains your facial expressions," she gasped between laughs. "Oh, I love you. That's hilarious and I feel even more thankful to have you as a friend."

I pushed her leg with my foot. "Get up."

She stood, wiped the tears of laughter from her eyes, and hugged me again. "Seriously, I love you. Thank you for being my friend."

I gave her a peck on the cheek and said, "You're welcome. Now, back to folding."

We folded in silence for a time, before I finally caved due to the curiosity.

"So, he doesn't have any sexual desires?"

She shook her head. "According to him, he just never felt those urges. He's had sex a few times, but said it wasn't particularly enjoyable, and he doesn't have the desire to do it again. So, I respect his wishes and the others are more than happy to have more opportunities with me."

"Do you ever share a bed?" Their relationship was even more interesting now.

"We have, but not often. He's used to sleeping on his own, so it's a bit awkward for him."

"So, when you go out in public, on his arm, it's mainly for the public perception?" I asked.

"Well," she frowned. "That's a part of it, but remember he does have romantic feelings, so he truly does love me and enjoys being with me. Wow, that sounds conceited, but it's true." She chuckled softly. "Anyway, yes it's for the public perception, and sometimes he just likes to have me at his side instead of me walking behind him with one of the others."

"Knowing this makes me love you guys even more," I told her. "That's really great that you're understanding of him and don't let it affect your love or relationship."

"He's amazing," she breathed. "Just as fiercely loyal and loving as the others. Just in his own way."

The more I learned about them, the more I couldn't understand how anyone could hate them. They were adorable.

"Did I tell you how I started working for him?" she asked.

I shook my head.

"He made a bet with me and beat me in a videogame to force me to start working for him," she said, a warm smile on her face. "Best thing to ever happen to me."

"That's so a-dork-able," I said with a smirk.

"Oh! Don't forget we have to go dress shopping tonight for the fundraiser," she said suddenly.

I glared. "I can't believe you're forcing us to go with you."

"It'll be fine," she said. "I'll keep the vultures away from you." She drew an x over her heart. "Cross my heart."

"Mmhmm," I said.

"I think we should get matching dresses," she suggested.

"I love you, but I'm not going to a high society function wearing matching dresses."

She pouted. "Fine. Spoil sport."

Laughing, I shook my head at her. "I will do almost anything for you, hun, but matching dresses is not one of them."

"Matching bracelets?" she asked.

I nodded. "I'll wear matching bracelets."

She smiled wide and I threw a sock at her. She ducked, mouth dropped, and threw the shirt in her hand at me.

I laughed and we soon devolved into a mess of clean clothes thrown all around instead of folded. And that was how Alexi found us, shaking his head with a soft sigh.

One look at Amelia, and we both teamed up to start throwing things at him instead.

Chapter 21

Amelia

"I better have a drink in my hand within two minutes of exiting this limo," Erina grumbled.

I snickered softly and Stephan gently pinched my side in reprimand.

"Don't laugh at your friend's discomfort," Stephan chastised.

"They brought it on themselves," I reminded him. "This is their payment to me."

"There's a lot of talk about debts, payments, etcetera. I think after this event, we should all be completely even," Marlee said. Brian squeezed her with a soft smile, clearly amused by all of this.

Brian wore a custom-made tuxedo with a silk bow tie, while Marlee wore a breathtaking silver ballgown with a plunging neckline and intricate beading. Her hair was styled in loose waves that cascaded down her back.

Connor wore a navy blue suit with a red tie, while Erina wore a dazzling red gown that shimmered with every move she took. Her hair was styled in an elegant updo, and her makeup was flawless, as always.

My dress was a stunning emerald green dress that hugged my curves perfectly with a plunging neckline and a thigh-high slit on one side. After wearing the dress that night at the casino, I'd learned that I liked the one-sided slit. My brand-new diamond necklace with a large solitaire emerald in the center glistened under the lights and cost more than any other necklace Stephan had given me. He said it was the first of many replacements for the ones that had been lost in the explosion.

"We will be sure to get you a drink as soon as we enter the room," Connor promised. "You're not the only one who's going to need one." He tugged at his tie, loosening it, but Erina immediately righted it.

"Where are your other husbands?" Marlee asked Erina and I.

"Shea, Forrest, and Dane are already there, making sure it's safe before we arrive," Stephan answered.

"Arcadio is keeping Hunter company at the house, watching the kids, and probably playing videogames togeth-er," I said.

"Blain and Damien are at the event already, too," Connor said. "Not that I don't trust Shea and the others, but it doesn't hurt to have more eyes able to spread out around the large building."

"Alexi is playing games with Arcadio and Hunter and watching Melina," Erina said. "They all developed very close friendships after our three months together at the beach resort and we thought it was a great way to kill two birds with one stone. They get a guys' night while also taking care of the children."

"You know my mom is probably stealing all three kids and hogging them for herself," I said with a soft laugh.

We arrived at the largest museum in the state where the fundraiser was being held. The museum was over one million square feet and often held events for the rich and famous. The fancy museum building was an architectural masterpiece that exuded elegance and sophistication. The exterior was made of smooth, white marble that gleamed in the sunlight, while towering columns supported the roof with iron designs around the columns and in the upper corners, creating a grand entrance. The museum building was the perfect location for a high-end event. It embodied the essence of luxury and sophistication, with a sense of history and culture that added to its charm. It was truly a feast for the senses, and an unforgettable experience that left a lasting impression no matter how many times I'd been to see it.

A red carpet led from the curb up into the front doors of the museum and dozens of reporters waited along the sides of the carpet to take pictures and shout out questions in hopes of getting an interview from the attendees.

"Ready?" Stephan asked and held out his hand.

"Nope, but I'll be better once we're inside," I said. I hated the flashing cameras and shouting reports and journalists. It was too much to deal with as you walked to the building.

"Just smile and wave," Erina reminded me.

"I'm not a penguin," I grumbled, trying to make a joke to ease my nerves.

Marlee and Erina both rolled their eyes simultaneously.

"Eye roll jinx!" I shouted, and laughed loudly at my own joke.

The limo door opened, our driver waiting patiently for us to climb out before he'd drive the limo to the nearby parking lot to wait for us to finish.

Stephan stepped out, adjusted his suit, and turned with his hand out to assist me with getting out.

Thankfully, this was an SUV limo, so I didn't have to worry about standing up, just stepping down. I set one of my hands in his and held my dress as I climbed out to prevent stepping on it.

The camera flashes were blinding and I had to remind myself to look down first to regain my vision.

Once I was steady on my feet, I dropped my dress, linked my arm through Stephan's, and looked up at him with an adoring smile.

"Good?" he asked.

I nodded. "Yes, thank you."

He kissed my cheek and began walking down the carpet, being sure to walk at a slow enough pace I wouldn't fall in my heels, even though they were low. One time, the carpet had bunched in a spot and the event employees hadn't noticed, and I'd tripped on it. That had been headline news for two days.

"Mr. Moriarty! Any word on the terrorist organization that destroyed your building?" one reporter yelled out.

Stephan and I smiled and waved, pausing to pose randomly as we made our way past them all, not answering any questions.

When we made it to the entrance, I turned back to see how Erina and Marlee were faring.

Both walked with extreme confidence, smiling and moving elegantly. Was I as elegant? I didn't think so.

The fundraiser was held in the grand ballroom with towering ceilings and walls adorned with gold and crystal accents. The room was filled with the sound of clinking glasses and the soft murmur of conversation. Waiters in black tie attire passed around trays of champagne and hors d'oeuvres while guests mingled and networked.

The center of the room was dominated by a large dance floor where couples twirled and swayed to the music of a live band. The band would play a mix of classic and contemporary tunes to please the diverse crowd.

Stephan led me straight to the nearest bar and ordered drinks for our entire group.

The ceilings were incredibly high, with intricate moldings and decorative details. Crystal chandeliers hung from above, casting a warm and inviting glow over the room. Large, ornate mirrors lined the walls, creating a sense of depth and grandeur. The ballroom was decorated with extravagant floral arrangements and towering centerpieces, with bursts of color and texture that added to the luxurious ambiance. I scanned the room, taking in the breathtaking chandeliers, the intricate floral arrangements, and the richly dressed attendees. Everywhere I looked, there were designer gowns, expensive jewelry, and perfectly coiffed hair. The place oozed with money from every seam.

"Those vultures get louder every event, I swear," Marlee huffed as she joined me at the bar.

I patted her arm and smiled. "You made it safely, that's what matters."

"Here's your drink," Stephan said and handed a bourbon on the rocks to Erina.

"You remembered," she exclaimed as she took it and sipped it.

Stephan nodded. "I try very hard to remember people's favorite drinks. It is one of the few things that everyone enjoys." He handed out the drinks to everyone else, handing me mine last.

I took it, and after a big drink let out a huge, happy exhale. "So tasty."

"Mr. Moriarty," a deep male voice said.

I knew that voice, it was the mayor.

"Mayor, I didn't expect to see you here," Stephan said politely.

"Do your cheeks hurt by the end of the night?" Brian teased me.

I hadn't even realized that I'd already plastered on my smile when the mayor walked up. I set a hand on his shoulder and laughed. "Too true, sir. Too true."

"Oh, there you are Mrs. Moriarty," the mayor said and turned to face me.

I dipped my head. "Mr. Mayor, it's nice to see you again."

"I hope that means you'll be voting for me in the upcoming election," he said and gave me a huge, politician's smile.

That fake, boisterous laugh left me again. "Oh, Mayor. You are too funny. If you'll excuse me, I need to make my way around the tables. Husband, will you join me?"

Stephan shook hands with the mayor. "I'll see you around, Mayor."

"Don't forget to vote," he said as we all walked away.

"Dear God, I don't think I've ever seen such an amazing performance," Erina teased and clapped softly.

"Oh, you haven't seen anything yet," Stephan said with a chuckle. "Wait until you see her talking to some of the other wives."

"And I thought angels didn't walk on Earth," Forrest said as he looked me up and down.

I fanned my face and smiled. "Oh, sir, you are such a flirt."

He picked up my hand and kissed my knuckles. "Perhaps tonight I can show you how an angel should be worshipped?"

"I'm going to be sick," Erina whispered.

I tsked. "Sir, you can't worship angels. That's blasphemy."

"Then how about I worship a goddess, because that is surely what's before me," Dane said from behind me. His large, warm hand rested against my lower back as he leaned forward and placed a kiss on my cheek.

"Are they like this everywhere you go?" Connor asked Stephan.

Stephan nodded. "Yep. Why? Did you think they were only like this at the house?"

Connor nodded.

Stephan laughed and shook his head. "Nope. They are like this every single place we go. Public or private."

"Do we have assigned tables?" Marlee asked.

"Right this way, ma'am. We'll lead you to your assigned

table," Forrest said, bowed, and spun around to walk us to one of the currently empty tables.

"Oh!" I exclaimed with excitement. "Since you're all here with me, we won't have others sitting with us. Oh my gosh, this night just got even better."

"Mrs. Moriarty!" a high-pitched female voice called.

I looked up and met eyes with the mayor's wife.

"Shit," I whispered. Taking a deep breath, I plastered on a smile, stood, and was immediately embraced by her.

She kissed each of my cheeks before holding me out at arm's length. "You look absolutely splendid! Were you at the beach recently?"

"Oh, yes. We've been staying at our beach resort," I answered, smiling wide as well.

Her smile disappeared and a look of concern replaced it. "How are you doing? When we heard what happened to your office building, it absolutely astonished us! If you need anything, you just let me know. I mean it. Permits, a place to stay, you just say the word and I'll whip my husband into action."

"You're so kind," I said and patted her hand that was still on my bicep. "We're doing well, though, thankfully."

She looked over my head at the table where Erina and Marlee were seated, snickering to each other about my current predicament. "Oh? Are these friends of yours?"

A frown formed before I could stop it because she one hundred percent, without a doubt, knew who they were. Quickly, I put my smile back on. "Yes, these are my best friends, Marlee and Erina."

She walked over and shook hands with Marlee first. "It's

a pleasure to meet you. Amelia is just a shining star and we absolutely love when she attends functions like this. Her aura just brightens up the entire room!"

"Yes, we love Amelia's aura as well," Marlee replied.

"No event is complete without Amelia," Erina said as she shook hands with the mayor's wife.

"Exactly how I feel! Sadly, she is often too busy to attend many of our functions," the mayor's wife said and gave me a pouty face. "Oh, I see Mr. Barken's wife. Please excuse me, ladies. I hope you have a wonderful night." She waved to us and glided across the room.

"And I thought Amelia was draining," Connor said as I took my seat.

Erina and I smacked his arms at the same time.

"Ouch!" he exclaimed. "I just meant that Amelia is always full of energy and it makes me feel tired. I wasn't saying anything bad about her. Geez."

"You're rude," I said, and took a huge gulp of my drink, which was now two-thirds empty.

Looking around, I spotted Shea against the wall. He was staring at me, conveniently. I raised my glass and jiggled it.

He nodded once, pushed off the wall, and headed to the nearest bar.

"Oh, that's a nice sign," Marlee said. "I wish I had guards with me I could do that with."

"Um, you can do it to my husbands and they'll get you refills," I reminded her.

"They won't mind?" she asked.

"Mar, you are family. They would literally kill a man who raised his hand against you. Getting you a refill is nothing."

"I can get you a refill if you want one," Brian said and stood.

A huge smile lit up her face. "Yes, please."

"Can you get me one, too, Brian?" Erina asked.

"What do you girls want?" he asked.

Stephan sat down beside me and answered before they could. "Bourbon on the rocks for Erina, and a lemon drop for Marlee."

"He's so good," Erina praised. "Can you teach Connor that?"

Connor scoffed. "I know what drink you like."

"And yet Brian's the one getting my refill," she taunted.

He groaned, stood, and clapped Brian on the shoulder. "Let's go, friend. I don't feel like being in the dog house tonight."

"Are you ever *not* in the dog house?" Brian teased.

"Rarely," Connor said.

Both laughed together as they walked towards the bar where Shea was heading back from.

"It's so nice to see them laughing together," Marlee said. "Those grumpy, old bastards finally found some happiness and it warms my heart."

"Do you refer to me as a grumpy, old bastard?" Stephan asked me.

"No, you're not a grumpy bastard," I said with a smirk.

He scowled. "I'm not old."

"You're not young either," Erina teased.

They served us our meals and we chatted quietly about random things between bites. A few people came over, trying to engage with Stephan, but his insistence on continuing to eat had them all leaving quickly.

After the dessert was served, the dancefloor began to fill and they started playing music again.

"Shall we?" Stephan asked, wiped his mouth with his napkin, and stood. He extended his hand to me and smiled.

I set my fork down, finished with my cheesecake, and stood. "If we must." I set my hand in his and he immediately pulled me forward and into a spin.

For some reason I couldn't comprehend, Stephan loved to dance at these events. It was like he was showing off, but he wasn't one to normally do that.

Having him to lead made my job a lot easier, plus we'd spent a lot of time practicing dances like the waltz and tango. I'd been embarrassed at how poorly I danced during one event and Stephan had taken my humiliation seriously, spending hours himself, plus making the others practice with me. A few nights while we were at the office, he would finish reading a document, turn on music, and start dancing with me.

It became something I looked forward to. Dancing with Stephan was fun, and if I did stumble, he was fast to cover it up, to make it look as though he were dipping me or it was his fault.

Chapter 22

Marlee

Watching Stephan whisk Amelia out onto the dancefloor put a huge smile on my face. She might act like she was put out coming to events like this, but she clearly enjoyed her time with Stephan.

"Would you like to dance?" Brian asked and stood; his hand held out as he bowed slightly.

Giddy excitement swirled in me. It had been a long time since we'd danced. I stood and he led me out into the growing number of people spinning around the dancefloor.

"You look absolutely stunning," he whispered as he twirled around, the dance movements as familiar as walking at this point in our lives.

As we continued to dance, I focused on the feel of his strong hand in mine, guiding me with precision and grace. Brian had always been an excellent dancer, a strong lead no matter what kind of dance it was. I let myself relax into the rhythm of the music, letting my body flow and sway with the beat.

The floor filled with other couples, all moving in unison to the music. The atmosphere was electric, with a sense of anticipation and joy that filled the air.

"You look even more handsome lately. Did you get work done?" I asked, a light teasing smile on my face.

His hand spread out on my lower back and he gave me a crooked smile. "I would have work done, but my wife would be very upset. For reasons I can't seem to fathom, she likes my appearance."

Amelia and Stephan spun by us and Amelia wiggled her fingers at me, her face flush with joy as they danced.

"Your wife has good taste," I said, focusing back on Brian. "She knows that true attractiveness comes from within and makes the exterior shine brighter."

"Is that why you glow like a goddess?" he asked, pressing our bodies closer together and letting his lips touch my ear as he spoke.

A shiver of desire ran through me and I straightened. "Sir, you are playing a dangerous game. If my husband were to witness what you just did ..."

He chuckled and said, "I'm fairly certain I could take your husband in a fight."

My head fell back as I laughed. "I'm fairly certain that fight would be a draw."

His lips pressed lightly against my cheek. "It makes me so happy to see you laugh."

As we twirled and spun, I felt a sense of freedom and lightness that had been missing for months, ever since Collman entered our lives. It was as though the music lifted me up and carried me away, allowing me to accept my worries and heaviness were now gone.

The waltz continued, and I lost myself in the dance. My partner's eyes met mine, and I felt a connection that was both intense and fleeting. It was as though we were in our own little world, separate from the rest of the party.

When the song ended, I thought we'd return to our seat, but he kept us on the dancefloor.

Connor and Erina joined us, and I found myself smiling wider as I watched my best friends with their husbands dancing alongside us.

Amelia spun by, this time with Dane as her dance partner. He whispered something in her ear that had her cackling with laughter.

"I'm glad that you ignored my warnings to keep your distance from the Moriarty's," Brian said, looking in the direction I was facing.

"They're growing on you, aren't they?" I asked, meeting his eyes.

"I won't admit it to them, but... yes. The joy you get when you're with Amelia was warming me up to her, but hearing how she protected you, and how she saved me, really settled it. Add in the past three months at the beach resort, and now my walls have been broken down even more. Stephan and Connor are, dare I say, my closest friends, next to you, of course."

"Of course," I said with a smirk.

"Seeing you laughing and enjoying your time with Erina and Amelia has truly made me the happiest about all of this," he continued. "For so long I felt like I was holding you back and that you needed something more, something I couldn't provide. And I was right. You needed some female friends, and these women are ideal even if I couldn't see that at first. I thought other mafia wives would be catty or try to use you instead of truly becoming your friends. These two have pleasantly surprised me."

"I was worried about that at first, too," I admitted. "I held myself back from truly developing a bond of friendship with them to see if they were just trying to use me. It took some time, but now I can see that they truly value me and my friendship. Amelia is always there for me and Erina. She's definitely the glue that held us together in the beginning. Now, our bond is solidified and even if you told me to stop being friends with them, I wouldn't."

Erina danced by with Damien as her partner, both smiling and dancing incredibly gracefully together.

Brian laughed and shook his head, drawing my attention back to him. "A year ago, I would have been furious to hear you say that, but now I understand. Those women complete you in a way that I couldn't."

"You aren't trying to leave me, are you?" I asked.

He spun me in a circle and dipped me as the song ended. "You couldn't get rid of me even if you tried, my love. You and are I one and the same, two halves of one soul in two bodies. Life without you would only be hell on Earth. No, I will never leave you."

He straightened back up, so we were both standing again.

I grabbed his face and kissed him deeply, my tongue sweeping across his. He hesitated for a moment, shocked by my public display, but his arms wrapped around me and he returned my kiss.

When we separated for air, he rested his forehead against mine while we both caught our breaths.

"I love you, Brian."

"I love you, too, Marlee."

"Ew, public displays of affection," Amelia teased as she spun around us with Forrest as her dance partner. "Get a room."

"I learned from the best," I teased back, my face warm with embarrassment, since Brian and I didn't really do public displays of affection often.

Brian slipped his arm around my waist and squeezed. "Come on, let's get a drink."

"Yes, please," I said, nodding.

He led me back to the table, pulled my chair out for me, and then went to the bar to get us drinks.

"You looked like you were having fun," Erina commented from the seat beside me. She fanned her face with her napkin, a happy smile on her flushed face.

"You look like you had fun, too," I said.

"I'm out of shape," she admitted. "I've got to get back to dancing more often."

I pulled my shoes off and noticed hers were off as well. "We need better dancing shoes, too."

She laughed and I joined her in the laughter.

Amelia and Forrest continued to dance for another song and then Shea took his place, the giant man dwarfing Amelia.

"I don't know how she does it," I said softly. "Or you for

that matter. Maybe I'm too old, but I can barely handle Brian. I don't know how you lot can handle so many men."

"Amelia is a beast," Erina said with obvious love in her tone. "She trains quite often, so her stamina is a lot better than ours. Plus, her men pay very close attention to her. They don't let her over work herself and will find excuses to get her to rest. Watch, she's starting to breathe heavier now that she's been dancing for so long. Guaranteed in the next minute, Shea will say something to her about needing a drink, lead her over to us, and then go get her a drink to bring back. He'll make it seem like he is stopping for himself when he is really doing it for her. My men do the same, but hers do it far more often. She wants to make them happy just like they want to make her happy, so sometimes they'll get stuck in a little bit of a loop, but that's when Stephan steps in to help convince her to stop or slow down. He's their voice of reason."

"You've really been paying attention to them," I commented.

"Well, we've been together for several months now and they aren't exactly private with their feelings and actions. Plus, it's been interesting to see how they work together. Those men are as different as you and I, yet they all work seamlessly together, especially where she's concerned. They will set aside everything to take care of her. It's really a lovely relationship."

As Erina predicted, a minute later Shea pulled Amelia off the dancefloor and helped her to her seat between us.

She panted, her face red, and a huge smile there. "Hey, ladies. Did you have fun?"

"We did," I replied. "Dare I say it, I'm glad you forced us to come to this event."

She pulled her shoes off and groaned loudly. "That's better."

"Here you go," Brian said as he set a drink on the table before me. "I'm going to go talk to a few business partners I see. Are you good here?" He set a hand on my shoulder and squeezed.

I nodded and patted his hand. "Yes, thank you. I need to rest my feet."

He kissed the top of my head and walked off to talk to a tall, slim man in a tuxedo with a bowtie.

"Who wears bowties?" Erina asked.

The three of us chuckled.

"Here you go, Kitten," Shea said and set a glass of ice water and another drink that looked like a lemon drop on the table before Amelia.

"Thanks, Oxie Loxie," she said and gave him a big smile.

He bent down and brushed his lips across hers. "I'm going back to patrol. Whistle if you need anything."

She nodded. "I'm going to rest my sore feet with the girls."

"Okay," he said and headed towards Dane who was talking to Forrest with a scowl in the far back corner of the room.

"Tonight has been fun," Erina said. "Not that I want to do this often, but it was a nice change of pace."

Amelia smiled smugly. "Thank you for coming with me. I knew this would be a better night with you two with me."

I leaned over and hugged her. "You're welcome. Thank you for being my friend."

Erina leaned over and put her arms around us both. "Ditto."

We separated and spent the next half hour drinking our drinks and talking about the people we saw. Amelia told us a little bit about some of the rich people there and Erina and I pointed out other people that we knew and what they were rich for. Then, we started gossiping about each of the groups, telling the little secrets we'd found out during our investigations. As expected, each of our mafia families loved digging up dirt on people. It was good to have on hand in case of blackmail emergencies. And after this evening, we had even more thanks to sharing it with each other.

I was about to wave to Shea for a refill when a man in the center of the area of tables drew a handgun from his jacket.

Amelia immediately shoved back her chair, grabbed Erina's arm and mine, and pulled us out of our chairs and down onto the floor, halfway beneath the table. "Get under the table," she ordered in a hissed whisper as a few women screamed.

"Just give me the wench I want and you are all free to go unharmed. If anyone tries to impede me, I will shoot the woman closest to me," the man said.

"Did either of you recognize him?" Erina asked in a hushed whisper.

Amelia and I shook our heads.

"Who is it that you're looking for?" the mayor asked.

"Amelia Moriarty," the man said.

From the corner of my eye I saw a few more men pull out

guns. Two of them aimed the guns at Shea and Dane who were together.

"What could you want with Mrs. Moriarty?" the mayor's wife asked.

"That's none of your fucking business," the man snapped. "Search the room. She's here somewhere."

"What do you want with my wife?" Forrest asked.

Amelia cursed beneath her breath.

Chapter 23

Amelia

Why was Forrest talking to the guy holding the gun? There were plenty of other people who could talk to him. If that guy was after me, they would know who he was, plus he referred to me as his wife, which gave it away even if he didn't know Forrest.

"Your wife owes me a debt," the man said. "A blood debt that I intend to take."

"Sir, you are not welcome here," the mayor said. "Please put your weapon away and leave."

The sound of flesh hitting flesh was clear, as was women's shouts of shock.

"Shut the fuck up, Mayor. Mrs. Moriarty, come out now or I'll kill the mayor's wife and her blood will be on your hands," another man said.

Shit. Shit. Shit.

I started to crawl out from under the table, but Erina and Marlee both grabbed my arms, stopping me.

"I can't let her die because of me," I whispered.

"You can't let him kill you either," Erina snapped.

"What's your plan?" Stephan asked the man. "You're going to shoot and kill her in front of all of these witnesses, and then what? You think you're going to leave here alive and be free? The police chief is here, among dozens of other high-profile witnesses. Did you think this plan through, or were you just set on trying to harm my wife and rational thought fled your tiny brain? Let me guess, you lot were part of the group that blew up my building downtown, weren't you?"

"How'd you guess that?" an unfamiliar male voice asked.

"Shut up, Stan!" the first gunman shouted.

Stephan scoffed. "Idiots. Attention! Everyone! I would like you to all bear witness to these men admitting that they are the terrorists who blew up Moriarty Tech's downtown building. Police Chief, I'm looking at you."

"I heard," a deep male voice answered.

A pair of black, shiny dress shoes stopped just in front of the table. A hand reached down and pulled up the tablecloth, exposing Marlee, Erina, and I. "Found you," a man with a huge scar down his cheek said and sneered. He reached down, grabbed my arm, and hauled me out from beneath the table and up to my feet. "Found her!" he yelled.

I could grab my dagger from my leg sheath and stab him, but not with so many of these types of witnesses present. That would totally put a damper on my reputation if they found out I carried a dagger on me and had absolutely zero qualms about stabbing a mofo.

He led me towards the center of the room where the first man I'd seen pull a gun stood, he was still facing Stephan and Forrest, the mayor on the ground by him clutching his bleeding head, and the mayor's wife sitting with her husband, tears making her mascara run down her face.

"There you are, bitch," the man snarled.

"I'm sorry, I don't think I've ever met you," I said sweetly. "Did I hurt you in a previous life or something? Fairly certain I had to have done something drastic for you to refer to me with such a rude and unkind word."

"You know what you did!" he snapped. "Angel Eyes did all he could to protect you and you repaid his desire with blood!"

Technically it had been buckshot, but I wasn't going to split hairs.

"Unhand my wife this instant," Stephan said in a deadly calm voice, "or I will be forced to protect her."

Two more men who were obviously part of the idiot's group, with handguns drawn approached, circling us.

"What do you think you're going to do, Mr. Moriarty?" one of the men asked. "You rich snobs, bosses with no real-life experience, have no idea how to handle yourselves in situations like this. You would do well to shut up and accept your wife's fate."

"You don't know anything about me," Stephan said calmly, "which I suppose works well for me in this situation."

Calm Stephan was deadly Stephan. I didn't want him to get hurt, though, and knew he wasn't carrying a weapon. Shea and the others were, but not Stephan. He was skilled in hand to hand combat, but I also didn't want him to give any secrets away to the aristocratic people in the room. We didn't need anyone here to know that he truly was part of the mafia and, I feared, if he engaged with these men everyone would see who he truly was. Not just the sweet technologically smart, business man, but someone who was capable of killing people without hesitation.

"Sweetheart," I said gently, "perhaps you should listen to these men. I'm sure the gunman and I can talk things out. He clearly has developed a misunderstanding about something."

"You fucking bitch. You know what you did!" he shouted and aimed his gun at me.

The moron was right next to Stephan, his gun in front of Stephan's chest.

Stephan grabbed the man's arm, wrenched it to the side, and took the gun from him. He hit the man in the head with the butt of the gun, stunning him and forcing him to his knees.

The other men started to raise their weapons, but Shea, Dane, and Forrest sprang into action.

The man holding me released his grip as he tried to draw his gun from his jacket. Without thinking, I punched him in the face and swept his legs out from under him. He hit the ground and still reached into his jacket.

Stephan was suddenly there, gun aimed at the man's face. "Don't," he hissed, his face full of fury and indignation.

The man froze and then slowly raised his hands up by the side of his head. "Okay."

I bent down, reached into his jacket, and withdrew his gun.

Several security guards and cops ran into the room, took the men, and put them in handcuffs. One of the cops took the gun from me and the other from Stephan.

"Thank you, Sergeant," Stephan said as he handed the gun over.

"Do you need an ambulance, Mr. Moriarty?" the officer asked.

Stephan shook his head then looked at me. "Are you injured?"

"No, I'm good. Thank you." I stepped forward and hugged him.

Stephan hugged me back and exhaled. "Thank goodness."

"Amelia," Marlee gasped as she and Erina ran over to me, both still barefoot, and hugged me between them.

"I'm okay," I said as I patted their backs. "Stephan protected me."

The mayor and his wife left with the cops to go to the hospital.

Several people came over to check on me and praise me for protecting myself. Many more praised Stephan.

Once again, Stephan had saved me. If he were one of my other husbands, I'd show him how thankful I was in a carnal way. Since Stephan drew the line at fully clothed cuddling and very light kisses on the lips or cheek, that wasn't going to happen. I enjoyed the cuddles and light kisses he occasionally gave me, since it was something he didn't do with anyone else. It was something special he shared with only me. At first when I'd found out he was asexual I thought it would be hard for me, but any affection he gave me was more than enough. Being at his side, being in a relationship with him was more than I ever hoped to have obtained. So, instead, I would need to find a gift or something to express my gratitude. Not that he expected it or anything, but I *wanted* to find something for him.

"Are you sure that you're okay, babe?" Dane asked as he came up behind Marlee.

I stepped out of Marlee's arms and let Dane hug me. "Yes, I'm fine. But perhaps now is a good time to head home. That's more than enough excitement for one fundraiser evening for me."

"I agree," Marlee said. "I'd like to have a drink on the couch while we watch a comedy."

"The limo is headed this way now," Shea advised as he pulled me out of Dane's arms to hug me, nearly squashing me in the tight embrace.

"Do I have to go to the police station?" I asked with my face buried in Shea's massive and warm chest.

"No," he answered. "I'm sure we'll have to write a statement to give the cops, but there were enough witnesses here, plus the police chief, that you won't need to go to the station."

I exhaled and sagged against him in relief. "Great. I like Marlee's idea of drinks and comedy. Maybe some snacks, too."

"Come, let's go get into the car," Stephan said and held out his hand.

Even though our relationship was public, we still tried to ensure that when cameras were present, I was on Stephan's arm. None of us minded.

I linked arms with Stephan and squeezed his. "Thank you for protecting me."

He looked down at me, a serious expression on his face. "I would have killed them if there hadn't been so many witnesses. I can't believe they were so stupid as to show up to try to harm you at an event like this. Collman clearly had a large following of absolute morons."

"Good thing you haven't slacked on your training," I teased.

The anger dissipated and he smiled. "Yes. It is definitely a good thing I have been vigilant about my training even while lounging on the beach most of the time these past few months."

"I think running on the beach helped. Running on sand is *hard*." I'd huffed like it was my first time running after just half a mile on the beach the first time. Now, I could run for a few miles, but it still sucked. I absolutely, one hundred and twenty percent, without a doubt hated running.

Shea walked in front of us with Dane and Forrest on either side, shielding us with their bodies. Were they worried there were more from that group who might try to shoot us out here?

Their worries were unnecessary as we all made it into the limousine without incident.

The ride to the airport was silent, as was the flight on our jet, and the drive to the resort.

"Mama!" Paige yelled when she saw me walk in.

Mom sat on the floor with Paige, Callen, and Melina, playing blocks with them.

Arcadio, Alexi, and Hunter sat on the couch playing a videogame.

Arcadio set his controller down and walked over. "Welcome home. We didn't expect you back this early."

"There was an... incident," I said.

His smile disappeared. "What happened?"

Alexi walked over to hug Erina and checked her for wounds. "Why are you carrying your shoes?"

"Lots of dancing. I'm fine. I wasn't injured at all," she said and kissed his cheek.

"I'll go get snacks and drinks," Shea said. "Dane, come help carry them."

"Coming," Dane said, tossed his tuxedo jacket on the back of the couch, and followed Shea towards the kitchen.

"The morons who blew up the office showed up to try to kill Amelia," Stephan told Arcadio.

Mom laughed. "You've really got to stop pissing people off."

I glared at her as I squatted down to hug Callen and Paige. "Shut up, Mom. You're one to talk."

"True," she said with a laugh. "I had quite a few death threats when I was with Stanley."

"The apple doesn't fall far from the tree on either side," Stanley said as he walked out of the hallway and out to the living room.

"Stanley! What are you doing here?" I asked.

"Am I not welcomed even after I helped save your asses?" he asked with an arched brow.

I rolled my eyes.

"You're always welcome in our homes," Stephan said.

"Wonderful. Well, I came to let you know that I've taken over Angel Eyes' territory permanently. I think it's time I come out of retirement and take back what was mine," Stanley said. "My family members reached out to me in droves, begging me to return and reform the family. Now that you have things under control here, it seemed like the perfect time."

"You're going back to be a mafia boss?" I asked, eyes wide.

"And I'm going with him, with Randolph as well, of course," Mom said and stood, putting her arm around Stanley's back.

"We'll be just a phone call and quick flight away if you need us, and we expect weekly videocalls so that we can see our grandbabies and ensure they remember us," Stanley said.

"I expect you to attend every other holiday with us," I added.

He smiled and said, "That sounds lovely."

I stood and hugged them both. "Thank you for everything you've done."

"You're welcome, sweetheart," Mom said as she hugged me. "You've grown into quite the woman. I'm proud of you. Now, just remember to keep these boys in line and do whatever Stephan says."

"Wow, way to show favoritism," Dane said and folded his arms across his chest as he reentered the room.

Mom waved her hand at him and he immediately set the tray of snacks he had brought down and went to hug her. "Take care of my girl. I'll cut your favorite hand off if you let her get hurt."

"Yes, ma'am," he said with a wide smile, not at all perturbed by her threat.

"Don't forget to invite us to the house warming when your new place is finished being built," Mom ordered Stephan as she hugged him.

"You'll be the first person I notify once it's finished and can help pick the house warming date," he said.

"Wow!" I gasped.

Mom stuck her tongue out at me and finished her hugging rounds, leaving the children for last. "Be good for your parents. Nana will see you soon."

"Bye, Nana," Paige said, and sniffled.

Arcadio picked her up and she buried her face against his shoulder to hide her tears.

Mom and Stanley left and reality hit me. Soon, we would all leave and go to our new homes. This was just the first step in that process.

I didn't want it to end. Not yet.

"Let's pick the comedy!" I shouted to Marlee and Erina.

They had matching frowns, which I assumed was because they had the same realization.

"Yes, let's," Marlee said, grabbing the controller.

Marlee, Erina, and I cuddled on the couch together, laughing at the silly romantic comedy we had turned on. Paige, Callen, and Melina crawled all over us, occasionally stolen by one of their fathers. We ate dessert, drank prosecco, and had one of my favorite nights ever together.

Yes, things were going to be changing soon, but our bonds were never going to fade. Of that, I was certain.

Chapter 24

Erina

"What do you think, love? Is it to your liking?" Connor asked as he stepped up behind me, his arms wrapping around my waist.

Our new house wasn't a house ... it was a castle! And I was one thousand percent okay with it.

Okay, the *outside* was a castle and two of the rooms were very similar to a castle, but the rest was contemporary opulence.

As I stepped through the grand entrance of my new house, I was greeted by a magnificent foyer adorned with an iron and crystal chandelier that illuminated the marble floors. The walls were lined with intricate moldings and frescoes depicting scenes from ancient mythology. Walking through the hallway, I entered my luxurious living room, which boasted floor-to-ceiling windows overlooking our vineyard. Plush, burgundy, velvet sofas and armchairs were arranged around a marble fireplace, and a grand piano stood elegantly in the corner, beckoning to be played, though only Alexi could play anything other than *Chopsticks* on it.

Next, I ventured into the opulent dining room, where a massive mahogany table was set for fifteen. A chandelier hung above the table, casting a warm glow on the intricate silverware and fine China. The room was adorned with antique tapestries and paintings, adding to the sense of grandeur. This room would definitely be used when meeting with business partners and those we wanted to impress, but not for our own dining. That room was on the opposite side of the kitchen, with a circular table just large enough to seat ten, a centerpiece of fake flowers so we would never have to change them out.

I continued my tour into the library, which was lined with shelves upon shelves of leatherbound books. An ornate wooden desk was situated in the center of the room, surrounded by comfortable leather chairs and a cozy fireplace.

Finally, I made my way to the master bedroom, which was designed for royalty. A massive four poster bed with plum silk sheets was the centerpiece of the room, large enough to fit all of my husbands and I at once lying side by side A luxurious sitting area with plush armchairs, a fireplace, and a white fur rug provided a relaxing retreat off to the side of the room with twin French doors that led to a patio with views of the garden. Warm sunlight filtered into the room through the curtains on the doors, making me feel relaxed and safe at the same time. The en-suite bathroom featured a spa-like atmosphere with a jacuzzi, marble shower, and gold-plated fixtures.

As I basked in the lavishness of the interior, I couldn't help but feel grateful for the hard work and dedication of my husbands that brought us to this level of success.

"Ready for the best part?" Alexi asked, a sly smirk on his handsome face.

I nodded. "Yes, please." My heart beat faster, thinking they were going to strip and show me some kinky additions I hadn't noticed on my initial inspection.

Alexi walked over to the large wooden armoire, pushed one of the knobs in, and the entire thing swiveled to the side.

My mouth dropped as I realized they had installed secret passageways into the house. "No way!"

Connor chuckled. "We know you like to tease Amelia, but we also know that you love the idea of secret passageways, especially if it's one more way that we can provide protection to our girl."

They were correct, I definitely wanted any additional means possible to keep my baby girl safe.

The interior was dimly lit, with emergency lighting showing the way. The passageway seemed to wind on endlessly, and I soon found myself in a large chamber, with high ceilings and intricate carvings covering the walls. In the center of the room stood a massive oak door, adorned with ornate brass handles and an electronic keypad.

As I approached the door, I couldn't help but wonder what secrets it held. Was it a safe room? An armory? The exit to another part of the castle?

"Code?" I requested.

"Our anniversary," Connor answered.

Without a moment's hesitation, I input the code, and with a loud creak, the door slowly swung open.

Inside, I found myself in a grand library, with towering shelves filled with hundreds of books, their spines letting me know the collection ranged from classics to things such as *Introduction to Business*, plus there were what appeared to be mysterious artifacts. The room was dimly lit by flickering candles, casting long shadows across the walls. Upon closer inspection of the artifacts, I quickly realized that they were fakes, most made of plastic.

"We thought it might entertain Melina when she was a little older to play with the items here, especially should things go down that required us to send her here," Damien explained in a soft voice.

As I made my way through the stacks, I couldn't help but feel like I had stumbled upon a secret world, hidden away from the rest of the mansion, despite knowing it was designed by my husbands for our daughter, it gave me a thrill and I couldn't wait to explore more of the castle's hidden passageways and secret chambers.

"This is ... perfect," I whispered and spun around with a wide smile to face my husbands. "You really thought of everything."

"You haven't seen the best part yet," Blain said and walked over to the large table at the center of the room, surrounded by plush leather chairs. He tapped the table three times. To my utter surprise, it split apart and a keyboard and screen slid up out of it. "This way, if you're stuck here, you can use it to communicate with Amelia or Marlee, to request help or chat, or whatever you want."

Tears spilled from my eyes and sobs forced me to clutch my stomach. "I ... I fucking love you all so much. How did I get so lucky?"

Damien rushed over and wrapped me in a hug. "We're the lucky ones. You're the only woman in the entire world who understands us and puts up with all of our insanity. You are our goddess, the only creature, next to Melina, who matters to us. I know I've said it before, but I will lay down my life to keep you smiling."

I thought about teasing him and asking if he'd been taking tips from Amelia's men, but didn't want to upset him. So, instead, I simply kissed him deeply, letting my tongue sweep across his and show him how happy those words made me.

He groaned in the back of his throat, his hold on me tightened, and I felt his immediate reaction.

"No screwing in the safe room," Connor said, though when I glanced at him, I could see he wasn't unaffected by our display.

"We've got to christen it, don't we?" I asked with a sly smile.

Alexi tsked. "Naughty, wife. No, we can go christen the bedroom if you'd like, though." He grabbed my wrist and pulled me from Damien. "Unless you'd like us to pin you against the wall in the secret passageway and have our way with you there?"

Oh, that did sound like a lot of fun. "Did you install chains I didn't see?" I asked and ran a finger down his chest.

"Those come in next week," he said and kissed my cheek. "I've got a separate room, hidden from visitor's sight, full of fun toys and contraptions, but it isn't fully ready yet. Once it is, we'll take you down there and show you the pleasures we have in store."

I pouted and stepped back from him. "Tease."

"How quickly do you think Amelia will find that room?" Connor asked with a sideways smile.

Blain threw back his head as he laughed. "Minutes. We all know that woman has an insatiable desire to find secrets and bring them to light. And yet, she's one of the few people I don't have any hesitation in bringing into this house."

Connor sighed. "I wanted to hate her so much, *so* much. But she's so damn likeable! It's impossible and yet she just skips into your life and is like, 'sorry I'm here now and you're going to like it,' and she isn't wrong!"

Laughter boomed out of me and I had to bend over to clutch my stomach as my husbands expressed exactly my same feelings I had about one of my best friends. "I told you!"

"We didn't believe it, but our time at the beach opened our eyes very quickly," Damien said. "Her men aren't too bad either."

"Did you measure dicks?" I asked and put my hands on my hips. They'd squabbled over who was better at every game, activity, and everything in between. I wouldn't doubt that they'd also dropped trousers and compared.

Connor's eyes narrowed. "Why are you interested in other men's dick sizes?"

I walked over to one of the bookshelves and thumbed through the titles. "Oh, I'm not. I already know how big the others are from Marlee and Amelia's accounts, but I was wondering if they were telling the truth or not."

Honestly, I didn't care if Amelia and Marlee lied about their husbands' dick sizes. I was curious if the men had really compared sizes.

Swinging back around, I watched Damien's cheeks redden as he turned his head away.

My mouth dropped. "Oh. My. God. You *totally* did!"

"We were really drunk!" Damien shouted then pointed at Connor. "He egged us on, making bets with Stephen that *his* men couldn't possibly be bigger than us."

Squatting down, I kept one hand against the bookshelf as I tried not to die with laughter. They'd actually done it! I was going to call Marlee and Amelia and tell them. We were going to all die laughing from the discussion.

"S-So wh-who was biggest?" I asked between gulps of breath.

"It doesn't matter," Blain said indignantly and folded his arms across his chest.

Oh, snap! That meant it wasn't them.

"It was Shea, wasn't it?" I asked with a smirk. Amelia had bragged about him, but I thought she'd been grandstanding.

All of my husbands jerked their heads up to look at me.

"How'd you know?" Connor asked.

"I told you, we girls talk. Amelia told us how big he was and how it takes her time to get accommodate him. We thought maybe she was just, you know, *tighter*, but clearly that's not the case. Damn, I totally lost the bet on that. I owe her a new purse."

"Wait, you made a bet? How were you going to prove it?" Blain asked, his brows furrowed.

I smiled wide and waved at them. "I just proved it."

They looked at each other and then back at me. A few seconds later, they all exploded with laughter.

Well, at least they saw the humor in it, too.

Chapter 25

Marlee

Our new house looked like an average mansion that you might see a celebrity own. At least from the outside.

Anyone who came to visit would walk around the beautiful, modern house, admire the pretty designs, lights, and decorations. What none of them saw was the two stories *below* the house.

Those two substories were the true, main house. That was where their bedrooms, offices, living rooms, armory, command center, and housing for their most loyal family members were.

This time when the rooms had been designed, Brian had put my bedroom right next to his, so that it was easier to step through the adjoining door when I needed to leave. He hoped it would allow for more time together. I agreed to go to bed with him each night and leave if it became too much for me to handle.

One of the many perks of having stayed with Amelia, Marlee, and their men was that my husband witnessed other ways of marriages working. Ones where they, like us, craved as much time together as possible.

We'd not hired a laundry service, deciding to follow Amelia's example and do the laundry together as one more excuse to spend quality time together. We had put the laundry room right next to our bedroom to make it even easier.

Amelia had tried her hardest to figure out how to get to our lower levels, at the approval of Brian, and still hadn't managed to figure it out. She'd pouted for hours about it, but we finally showed her the secret and that had made her incredibly happy.

We were still working on replacing our wardrobes and all the things we had purchased over our lifetime that we couldn't live without.

I had forgotten how much I used my booze spoon with the meddler on one end until I didn't have it anymore.

Amelia and Erina had also purchased silly and cute kitchen contraptions for me like a tea spoon shaped like the loch ness monster so it's cute little head poked out of your tea while you drank it. And a crab that you put on the edge of your pot that held your spoon in its raised claws. They'd both laughed about it for five minutes straight after showing me how to use it.

My favorite gift was the wine bottle opener shaped like a little bat. Every time I used it, I pictured my best friends and it made me smile.

At their urging, I had also restarted my therapy sessions. My paranoia still wasn't gone even though Angel Eyes was gone and even I knew it wasn't healthy to be constantly looking over my shoulder, heart pounding.

The first night in the new house, I'd woken with a scream, recalling the man who'd tried to kidnap me and sliding down the emergency exit. In my dream though, I'd lost my hold and was falling to my death.

Brian had rushed into my room, gun in hand, prepared to murder someone, but had quickly set the gun down and hugged and kissed me until I fell back asleep.

Things were getting better and I very rarely had night terrors or panic attacks.

The girls and I had set up a rotation of visiting each other's houses, a way to keep our husbands appeased, and still have plenty of visiting time together. Plus, it allowed us to have it on their calendars well in advance so nothing could be planned over it. Nothing could stop us.

That was a huge reason I had insisted on not just an outdoor, heated pool, but also a covered patio area with a large spa with more than a dozen jets. You could get a massage while relaxing in the spa at the same time.

"Are you ready to head over to the house warming party?" Brian asked as he adjusted his shirt cuff and entered my room.

I finished putting on my mascara and double checked the rest of my makeup. "Yes, I think I'm presentable now."

He squatted down behind me, looking at me through the mirror's reflection. He smiled and said, "Well, I'd definitely hit it."

I turned and smacked his arm. "Incorrigible."

Warm lips pressed against my temple as I stood. "Just for you, my love. Just for you."

Spinning around, I wrapped my arms around his waist and rested my head against his chest. "I love you, Brian. Thank you for giving me the life you have given me."

He squeezed me tight and rested his head atop my hair. "It's I who should be thanking you, Marlee. You are the one who has given me a true home, something I never expected to have when I took on this mantle. You are my one and only love, the light in my darkness."

Heat bloomed on my cheeks. "Right back at you." I tilted my head up and kissed him lightly on the lips. "You are my favorite person."

His smile widened and he said, "Can you say that again so I can get a recording of it and play it back for Amelia and Erina to hear?"

I swatted his arm playfully and stepped back. "Behave, sir!"

He chuckled and pinched my butt as he headed towards the door. "I am the epitome of well behaved and you know it."

I did. And I also knew that when he wanted to, he could be the silliest person and caused me to laugh even more than Amelia did.

"Let's go see our friends' house," he said and held out his hand.

I set mine in it and nodded. "I challenge you to find the secrets before me."

He winked. "Challenge accepted."

Chapter 26

Amelia

The new house was finally built. Six months after we had sent the design build to the company, we had our house ready to decorate and move into.

It took me three weeks to find furniture for all of the rooms and art to decorate the halls, and two more weeks to decorate each room with said furniture and art. Stephan had offered to pay for an interior designer to come, but I wanted to do it myself. Plus, the guys offered a lot of suggestions and help.

Marlee and Erina had moved into their places a month ago and once they left, the resort felt far too big and quiet.

In our new house, things were starting to fall back into our normal rhythm, and life was moving on.

We'd attended Marlee and Erina's house warming parties and it had been a blast. They were right about distance being good. Even though we talked by text and video often, being reunited in person was definitely a wonderful experience each time.

The final members of Angel Eyes' group had been captured. Stephan kept their fates a secret from me, which I was fine with. I assumed they were dead, but I only cared that they weren't going to continue to hunt me.

"Where are the napkins?" I shouted as I searched through the cupboards. Today was the day of our house warming and I was frantically trying to get everything ready.

"They are already on the table," Hunter said. "And you are supposed to be getting changed."

"I have to make sure everything is ready first," I explained.

Dane grabbed me from behind, his arms wrapping tightly around my waist, and rested his chin atop my head. "Babe, we've got it. Besides, these are just family coming. Now, go get changed and do your makeup and hair."

I touched my hair, which was frizzed out in different directions. "Oh, right. I didn't brush my hair yet today."

"Do you want some help getting ready?" Dane asked in a deeper voice, his hands dipping lower on my stomach.

Spinning out of his hold, I gave him a glare and pointed a finger at him. "None of that, mister! I'll go. You all just make sure all the drinks and plates and things are ready."

"We're on it," Dane said and saluted me.

I narrowed my eyes, but backed out of the kitchen and went to my room.

A new silver dress lay on my bed with matching sandals and a new diamond necklace. A small note lay atop it from Stephan:

Thank you for taking care of the new house. Here's a small token of my appreciation.
~Stephan

After a quick shower, I took the time to style my hair and do my makeup, spending as much time as I would if we were going to a gala or special event. Then, I put on the new gifts and stared at my reflection in the mirror.

The woman who owned a failing coffee shop that thought she was going to be single for the rest of her life would be insanely jealous of the woman in the mirror. It was hard to believe just how far I had come. Just how much my life had actually changed thanks to the men who had found me in that coffee shop. What would have happened if I had won the bet against Stephan and not worked for them? Would we still be here?

"Mama!" Callen yelled from a nearby room.

"Coming!" I yelled back.

There wasn't a single thing about the past I would change, because where I was right now, this present, was the greatest thing I had ever experienced.

As I walked down the hallway, I found not just Callen, but all of my friends and family, waiting in the foyer.

"Welcome to my home!" I shouted and spread my arms wide.

Erina and Marlee bombarded me with hugs and praises on my décor. I took Melina from Erina and pinched her adorable little cheeks, making her squeal and bat at my hands.

Connor and Brian even gave me hugs as they came inside. Alexi took Melina from me as he walked by and Damien and Blain gave me smiles, still not quite at the hugging stage yet. That was okay, we would get there eventually.

Mom stole Paige and Callen from Arcadio and Shea, patting them on the cheek before she began her exploration, a child on each hip.

"Your place looks lovely," Randolph said.

I gave him a hug. "Thanks, Dad."

He pinched my cheek. "I'm proud of you."

Tears pricked my eyes, but I blinked them away and smiled wide. "Thank you."

Stanley gave me a hug and started knocking on the walls.

Marlee and Brian started moving decorations and art slightly to the side before letting it all back down.

"What are you all doing?" I asked, head tilted to the side in confusion.

"Looking for your secret passageways. I know you put some in," he said and resumed his knocking.

"We're trying to find the secrets, too!" Marlee admitted.

I laughed and shook my head. "I'll give you the full secret tour after we eat. Deal?"

"I want that tour, too!" Erina shouted.

"Yes!" Marlee yelled.

"Fine! We'll do the main tour, eat, and then the secret tour," I agreed.

"It's not much of a secret if everyone knows," Shea grumbled.

"I'm not going to post the tour online," I said and rolled

my eyes. "It's important for all of our family to know the passageways for their safety."

He raised his hands in surrender. "Yes, boss."

I smirked and sashayed by him. "I like hearing you say that."

"Don't get used to it," Stephan teased. "You already have a nickname."

"What is her mobster nickname?" Erina asked. "I'm just Lady."

"Hey, that's my name, too," Marlee said and both laughed.

"This woman right here? This perfection of mafia talent? This is the Mobsterina," Forrest said.

I twirled, my dress fanning out as I did, and then curtsied. "At your service."

"Oh, my god. That is the perfect name for you!" Erina gasped.

"Babe, I want a better name," Marlee said, and pouted at Brian, who laughed and put his arm around her shoulders.

"Sorry, there's only one Mobsterina," I teased.

"And she is all we could ever hope for," Dane said, pressing a kiss to my cheek.

Yeah, this was the perfect life, and even though I knew I would never be the main character of any story, I was definitely living my happily ever after.

If you enjoyed this series and like paranormal romance, check out the complete Her Royal Harem Series at: www.book s2read.com/re

If you prefer contemporary books, check out Knot a Midlife Crisis at: www.books2read.com/KAMC

Don't forget to join my newsletter at: http://catbanks.co/ Newsletter

About the Author

Daisy Emory is the contemporary romance pseudonym for Catherine Banks, USA Today Bestselling Author.

amazon.com/author/daisyemory

About the Author

Catherine Banks is a USA Today bestselling fantasy author who writes in several fantasy subgenres and has multiple pseudonyms. She began writing fiction at only four years old and finished her first full-length novel at the age of fifteen. She is married to her soulmate and best friend, Avery, who she has two amazing children with. After her full-time job, she reads books, plays video games, and watches anime shows and movies with her family to relax. Although she has lived in Northern California her entire life, she dreams of traveling around the world. Catherine is also C.E.O. of Turbo Kitten Industries™, a company with many hats including being a book publisher and Etsy store full of nerdy fun.

facebook.com/catherinebanksauthor

amazon.com/author/catherinebanks

bookbub.com/authors/catherine-banks

9 781946 301758